MW00880473

Wounded Heroes

Anthology

Pamela Ackerson

Debra Parmley

Teri Riggs

Maggie Adams

Nia Farrell

A Rosa for Russell ~ Pamela Ackerson
PamelaAckerson.com @PamAckerson

Two Step, New Steps ~ Debra Parmley
DebraParmley.com @DebraParmley

Bringing Her Home ~ Teri Riggs
Teri-Riggs.com @TeriLRiggs

As Time Goes By ~ Maggie Adams
MaggieAdamsBook.com @AuthrMaggieAdms

Fallen ~ Nia Farrell
NiaFarrell.wordpress.com @AuthrNiaFarrell

Wounded Heroes Anthology

A Rosa for Russell by Pamela Ackerson
© Pamela Ackerson 2019

Two Step, New Steps by Debra Parmley
© Belo Dia Publishing 2019

Bringing Her Home by Teri Riggs
© Teri Riggs 2019

As Time Goes By by Maggie Adams
© Maggie Adams 2019

Fallen by Nia Farrell
© Nia Farrell 2019

Wounded Heroes Anthology © Pamela Ackerson 2019
All rights reserved.

No part of this book may be reproduced or utilized in any form by any means, electronic or mechanical, including photocopying or recording, or by any information storage and retrieval system, without permission in writing from the publisher.

Cover Design: Crystal Visions
Editing: Stephanie Taylor

Wounded Heroes Anthology

Five Degrees of heartwarming to melting stories —
Five stand-alone love stories with swoon-worthy
heroes that will leave you breathless from award-
winning International, USA Today, and Amazon
bestselling authors Pamela Ackerson, Debra
Parmley, Teri Riggs, Maggie Adams, and Nia Farrell.

* *A Rosa for Russell* ~ Who in their right mind *falls in
love* with the enemy?

** *Two Step, New Steps* ~ Wounded cop Len Yardley
doesn't expect to find love while he's healing from a
gunshot wound but the air force veteran can't help
falling for perky Leanne Bobbin who brings out his
protective instincts and makes him laugh.

*** *Bringing Her Home* ~ Can Thomas Raintree bring
home the woman he loves, but had to leave behind?

**** *As Time Goes By* ~ Blake's determined to find
out who killed his best friend, and his widow holds
the key ...not only to the murder, but also to Blake's
heart.

***** *Fallen* ~ An Army chaplain priest's faith is
tested when he falls for his PTSD therapist.

A Rosa for Russell

by

Pamela Ackerson

1864 Camp Sumter ~ Andersonville Prison

Boom!

A shot rang out and tore apart another precarious thread of hope. Rosa cringed.

"We've got another group coming in." the sergeant called from the open door.

"So much for my tea," Rosa commented to the soldier who sat down next to her.

He grunted and followed her out the door.

She joined the group at the entrance to the infirmary.

"Welcome to *Hell on Earth*, *boys*," the soldier sneered.

He moved aside. Men carried Union soldiers and unceremoniously plopped them onto available cots. The eyes of the injured, bloody men held fear and pain. Blood dripped onto the recently cleaned floor.

Her nose flared wide as one soldier was carried by; the reek of gangrenous flesh was strong and repugnant.

Rosa sighed. The memories of *Hell on Earth* would haunt her forever. She'd never be able to get the stench of death and destitution out of her mind or thoughts.

For those who would survive, she couldn't imagine what it would do to them. For those who wouldn't, was it a blessing? Her nightmares began the very first day she worked at the prisoner of war camp.

It was an emotional plague. She went home every night. She didn't have to survive, not in the same way they would. The broken choked pain from the prisoners, and useless death of her fellow Americans was her relentless torture.

It was reprehensible what they put these men through. Rosa prayed the Union prison camps were more humane.

The man snorted and helped carry in more wounded Union soldiers before returning to her. "I don't know how you do it."

He was newly arrived, and already ragged and hollow-eyed. She didn't even know his name.

"I've been here since February '64. The prison was built to accommodate relocated Union prisoners. It wasn't supposed to have more than 10,000 prisoners.

"They transferred me from the Confederate hospital in Americus. I arrived at Andersonville a few days before they started bringing in the soldiers."

He grimaced. "I'll be working in the towers."

She nodded and frowned. "By the end of this war, you'll be calling them *the walking dead*." She looked toward the commotion. Bodies were being shoved around, placed in corners, on the floor, and two to a bed.

3

A distant shadow darkened his eyes, and he let out an exhausted breath. "You've been here since the beginning?"

"Yeah. When I arrived, they hadn't finished construction before they started putting them in the prison pens. Like today, some of them were brought directly to the infirmary."

"Didn't they stop paroling prisoners because they returned to their troops to fight instead of going home?" he quietly asked.

She responded with a nod.

He looked out the window toward the pens. "When did the prison reach capacity?"

"Oh, after about three months? Or maybe it just felt that way. They expanded it to twenty-five acres in early July. Like I said before, it was only supposed to hold 10,000 men, but by mid-August, there was well over 32,000. The Yankees sleep under whatever they can. Some are lucky enough to build shebangs. The unlucky ones sleep under open skies."

"What's a shebang?"

"Makeshift covers. They use anything and everything they can get their hands on: wood pieces, ripped clothing, torn blankets."

The sergeant flipped his hand toward the doorway. "Andrews, help her in there for now."

He followed Rosa inside.

It didn't faze Andrews when they opened the wrappings around a wound on a Union boy's arm. After a quick assessment, Rosa confirmed it would need to be amputated.

The boy was barely conscious.

Several gunshots reverberated in the distance. Andrew's jumped at the sound.

Did he know that's what he'd be doing in the towers?

She shook her head. "Most likely some of the new prisoners trying to escape."

"What'd they call it? *Hell on Earth?*"

"That's what the prisoners call it. And appropriately so. Every time I hear a gunshot, I know someone has tried to pass the deadline. We'll either be burying more soldiers in the trench for trying to escape or treating their wounds."

She marked amputation on the boy's chart.

They moved to the next patient and continued down the line, soldier after soldier. She asked their names, marked the charts, recorded their injuries, and did minor ministrations until she obtained more medical supplies.

Rosa's heart clenched in her chest. "It's so futile. We're fighting dysentery, vermin, ticks, diseases, starvation, battle wounds…"

She finished cleaning a young boy's wound, cleaned his face and recorded a recommendation to extract the eye.

Such a useless waste of good men.

She walked to the next bed. Rosa immediately sensed the warmth above the soldier's body. It was an eerie feeling. She'd never experienced anything like it until she worked here at the infirmary.

Death so recent, she could touch the heat leaving his body.

Rosa pulled on the eyelid. His eyes were glazed with a milky grey.

She turned to a soldier in the corner, and flipped her hand and pointed outside.

"Do you know who this is?" Rosa asked the boy she'd just treated.

His voice broke, and his eyes watered. "My brother, Gabriel."

Rosa swallowed the lump in her throat. "I'm so sorry."

The boy grimaced and turned away.

They came and carried out the body.

Andrews asked as they moved to the next bed. "Nothing you can do for him?"

She took a deep breath. "No, he was gone."

Andrews watched them carry Gabriel to a cart and throw him on top. It was filled with bodies.

He gagged.

"You okay?"

He stared at the death on wheels, the telltale sign of his Adam's apple bobbed with each gulp revealing his distress. She couldn't reassure him. It wouldn't get better. At least not for a while.

The buzz of flies came through the open window.

Rosa saw him pale. "That's a sound I have nightmares about, too. It's enough to make me choke. I'm sure you've seen the creek separating Camp Sumter from the prisoners.

"It's supposed to supply the Union soldiers with fresh water. Unfortunately, it's become a cesspool of disease and human waste. I think the Confederate soldiers use it to bathe and relieve themselves. The Union soldiers were doing the same until they started getting sick.

"The water is too toxic. Some boil it. What else are they supposed to do? They figured out fast enough not to drink the water."

Rosa approached an auburn-haired young man. His battle-worn body looked defeated. But when she looked into his eyes, she saw pure determination.

She wondered how long it would take before he lost hope. She wrote down his name, Russell McNamara, and other vital information for his chart.

Andrews was called to help the other soldiers outside.

She concentrated on the wound. *Not good.* Stomach wounds were the worst. At least it was to the side under the ribs. She hoped it wasn't too deep or infected.

Her heart broke watching the man clench his teeth as she cleaned his wound. His chest pounded under her fingertips. Sweat beaded on his face and arms.

He spoke to her with a slight brogue accent. "I don't understand. Why would the buzz of flies cause nightmares?"

Amusement tickled her voice, and she moved his hair away from his face. "Have you been listening to my conversation?"

"Yes ma'am. I like the sound of your voice." He offered her a half-hearted grin. "You keep talking. I like it. Is it really so bad?"

A tear dropped down the edge of Rosa's cheek. "God help me, but I loathe going outside near the pens. Two minutes out there, and you'll be covered in ticks, fleas, and biting flies. The stench alone is enough to turn a person's stomach. All those flies."

She raised her hand in a semi-circle. "Between the two hills is a dark black swamp. It's where the soldiers dump…dump their filth and excrement."

"Oh, lass. I imagine there's a constant buzz from the flies and the maggots. Bet they're on everything."

Rosa nodded. "The buzz is so loud. I hear them in my sleep." Her eyes were unfocused, and she got lost in her own personal nightmare.

"A beautiful rose like you should never have to live with such sadness and horror."

Such a silly compliment, but Russell managed to break the guilty silence. Rosa didn't know what else to say.

She scoffed. "You're a big flirt. Trying to sweeten me up, aren't you?"

He winked. "What's your name, lass?"

"Rosa."

"Well, I'll be a monkey's uncle. A Rosa for Russell." He put his shaky hand out.

She shook it. "Nice to meet you, Russell."

"Who's that?"

She turned to see who walked into the room.

"Dorence Atwater. He's a prisoner but works here with us. He does the record keeping."

Russell snapped in disgust, "A traitor?"

"Goodness, no! He was just lucky enough to have an education and be useful." Heat flushed her face and sucked in a shaky breath. "I didn't mean it like that!"

"I know what you meant, my Rosa."

"He's a great help to all of us."

And she knew Mr. Atwater was doing much more than simple record keeping. She asked him one time why he kept two copies. She hadn't forgotten how nervous and fidgety he got when she approached him.

It took a few moments for her to realize he wasn't supposed to be keeping two records. She had no idea why, but she suspected he was doing it for his Union comrades and their families.

Well, no need for *her* to say anything...

***

Several days later, Rosa was treating a prisoner placed next to Russell's cot the night before. The boy didn't say a word. He watched Rosa attend to his injuries.

Russell asked, "How's he doing?"

Rosa jumped. "I thought you were asleep."

"I was but I don't —I haven't slept well lately."

"Understandable."

Russell whispered, "He said they tortured him."

She clenched her jaw. The boy's injuries weren't consistent with normal wounds. The medical supplies were practically nonexistent. Torturing the soldiers was absolutely unnecessary.

It just made her madder than a mule chewing on bumblebees.

"You bring in your own medicinal herbs, don't you?"

She nodded. If she hadn't known how to use medicinal herbs, it would've been much worse. The prisoners were living in despicable conditions.

"It's disheartening," Rosa's voice broke.

"What's disheartening, my sweet Rosa?"

Rosa shuddered. "Why torture them? Can you imagine how desolate and alone these prisoners feel? I couldn't handle the depression, and I'm not even a captive. I can't fathom how some of them have survived."

Sarcasm with a drip of amusement rang in his voice. "Actually, yes, I can imagine how they feel."

She sucked in a quick breath. "I'm sorry."

"Don't you worry your generous heart. We'll be fine." Russell looked over to the patient next to him. "Won't we, Rogers?"

The boy nodded.

"Okay, Russell. Now you're awake, let me look at your wound."

He rolled to his side so she could get a better look.

"He was with my company."

"Who was?"

"Rogers."

She bit her lip.

Russell grimaced. "He helped me when I needed it most."

Rosa nodded as she checked him.

"My brother…" His voice croaked.

She grabbed supplies and waited for him to continue.

"My brother was right next to me when we both were gut-shot. They got him in the face, too."

She watched Russell's chest rapidly quiver up and down. She put her hand on his racing heart.

"Wasn't much left of his head. I put him out of his misery."

Rosa tears crawled slowly down her cheek. A gut wound was the most excruciatingly painful way to die. But on top of a head wound…

Russell rasped. "My hand shook so bad, I would've missed if I used my pistol. The boy handed me his knife so I could send my Kev to the Lord."

Rosa sucked in a breath.

"It's how Rogers got the bullet. He put himself in harm's way so my brother wouldn't suffer."

"Oh, Russell."

He whispered, "I had to kill my own brother. I'm a *murderer*."

She looked toward the boy who was vehemently shaking his head. "He did what he needed to do. I don't know if I could've done it."

Russell's voice was broken. "My brother. He was a handsome man and well-liked. He loved to joke and be friends with everyone."

Rosa massaged his forehead. "Hush. You're getting yourself upset."

"He saw the Rebs and jumped in front of me to take the bullets."

"Shh…you're here now. It's over."

"Oh, lass, it's just beginning. I have a bigger fight here."

"I'm sorry. I truly am."

"Not your fault. You're doing what you can. You're saving a lot of Union soldiers."

She grunted. "Yes, to send them back to the pens."

"But they're alive."

"Are they?"

"Yes, my Rosa. It may be *Hell on Earth*, but we're alive. I still wonder though.

"I wake up sometimes in a cold sweat. Why? Why am I the one who lived and my brother met his maker? He was a good man."

Silent tears streamed down both of their faces. There was a clatter of boots outside the infirmary.

Rosa wiped her cheek and turned to see a glimpse of uniformed officers pass by.

He calmed himself down. After a few moments, he asked, "Do you know Captain Wirz?"

"Yes, of course I do. He makes his rounds to the infirmary almost every day."

"I haven't seen him."

He hissed when she pulled the wrap from his wound.

"I've heard things since I've been here. Is he as bad as the rumors say?"

Rosa mumbled, "I will not speak ill of the man."

She pushed gently on the bruised area.

Russell grunted. "It's getting cold at night."

"Typical for late October."

"They took my blankets and provisions when they captured me."

She nodded.

"What division were you in?"

"Pleasonton's Provisional Cavalry Division. I was captured at the battle of Mine Creek. Heard some people call it the Battle of the Osage."

"Where was that?" Rosa asked.

"Kansas." Russell winced. His breathing was labored. He silently dealt with the pain from her rubbing the raw wound. "Was part of Price's Raid," he continued. "How's the infection looking?"

"Much better. They're letting you go into the pens tomorrow."

He inhaled a shaky breath.

"I'll give you a poultice to take with you."

***

Russell became a regular visitor to the infirmary. She didn't know why he stuck in her thoughts. He was just another Union soldier.

The man had an unshakable, deep faith. It lighted his eyes. After everything this war had done to him, he still found a way to smile. Sometimes, she saw sadness reflected there. Most of the time, he looked for anything to stay positive. Rosa could take a few lessons from him.

She saw him one time, just standing in front of the infirmary, his eyes closed and facing the sun. She'd have to try it and see if it helped after a long, arduous day.

She was frustrated with him as well. He kept returning with injuries. Every other day, she treated him for something and gave him poultices and medication.

Supplies were limited. A few months back, instinct had her making more medications and poultices for treatments. Now, Rosa was glad she did it. Even still, it wasn't enough.

Russell wasn't being tortured. His injuries were consistent with getting into fights. She heard stories about the Irish and Scots liking to fight and wondered if it was true.

"You must love coming to see me at the infirmary."

He waved his hand over his face. "It's all a pretense so I can spend some precious time with you."

"Your eye is swollen shut. What'd you do? Why do you keep getting into fights?"

He clenched his jaw and shrugged.

"You're a stubborn man, Russell."

She saw the glittering defiance and determination reflecting back at her. His body was frail and defeated, but his inner strength shining in his eyes never wavered.

"Actually, my Rosa, I came in because I'm ailing. Got a fever and chills. Feeling a bit queasy, understand?"

She raised a questioning eyebrow. The man didn't have a fever. His infection from the wound was long gone, and he didn't look sick or pale.

"I am sick. I'm nauseated by the stink of the swamp and those wildfires are giving me a sore throat. I'm sick of the smell," his nose flared.

She imagined he was sick of it all.

"The smoke's not from wildfires." She frowned. "Union army's burning down Georgia. They started in Atlanta and are marching toward the Atlantic."

Russell grunted.

"I'm sure it makes you happy, burning down everything we cherish."

"No, it doesn't. But if that's what it takes to win…"

"Well, I declare!"

"Now don't go getting all mad at me. I'm here sick as a dog. I need medicine."

He opened his good eye and attempted a look of innocence. She laughed, shook her head, and handed him a jar and some herbs for brewing tonic.

Russell whispered, "Do you have some of the powder? It's working real good with the water."

She patted his shoulder. "It's in the jar."

Rosa grinned. Sodium hypochlorite was a life-saving discovery. Her father accidentally spilled some of the powder in the rain barrel and the water cleared. They were able to drink it and use it for watering the herbs.

It was a god-send.

***

Over the weeks, Russell came to the infirmary with all sorts of invented ailments. After a while, she figured out the medication wasn't for him. She heard rumors buzzing around from the Yanks who were admitted to the unit. Russell gave his extra medication to the Negroes. Dr. White was only around for the major issues, amputations, severe infections, and some diagnoses.

She took care of the minor complaints.

"I know what you're doing." Rosa cleaned another slightly deep cut on his arm. "It'll need to be sutured."

"I'll need…" His voice trembled.

"We're not allowed to treat them. Russell, you need to understand, we barely have supplies for the Confederate soldiers and the Union prisoners."

"The Negroes *are* Union prisoners and there's almost a hundred of them in this camp. They fought in this war for *our* country. They're men, not animals. It's a horrible, helpless feeling seeing them sick as they are with no one to care for them."

Rosa sighed and whispered in his ear, "I could get fired for this."

She desperately wanted to help all the prisoners. She gave Russell extra medicine, knowing full well what he was going to do with it. And he was willing to take the beatings…

"You're an angel, my Rosa. If it weren't for you, I'd have given up a long time ago. You restore my soul and remind me there is good in people. When this war is over…"

"When this war is over, you owe me a huge steak dinner."

"Well, then. That's something to help me sleep at night. Could you be sweet enough on me to let me give you a quick kiss on the cheek?"

She tapped his arm. "No. Now out you go. I've got men over there who are *truly* sick and need me."

She grinned. A kiss? The thought sent a cluster of warmth to her heart. Longing flared deep inside her.

Yes, she liked the idea of kissing Russell.

He looked back when he reached the door. He wiggled his eyebrows up and down. "It's Christmas in a few days. Perhaps it will be my gift from you."

***

Rosa fiddled with the necklace Russell made for her and placed it around her neck.

His face was swollen, and his jaw bruised. The doctor would be coming to check his leg. She suspected it was broken.

The grin on his face belied the pain he bore. "A Happy Christmas to you. I used cattails to make the necklace and…"

He handed her the matching bracelet, and she put it on.

"I will cherish this forever." She meant it. It would be hard to see him go when the war was over.

No, it wouldn't be hard. It would break her heart. God help her, she loved the man.

Who in their right mind *falls in love* with the enemy?

Her heart raced. She whispered, "I have something for you, too."

She handed him thick, oddly misshapen gloves. They looked like a small child crocheted them. The holes where he was supposed to slip in his hands were the size of a walnut.

Rosa couldn't help but see the amused look on his face. She saw him holding back the laughter. He clenched his lips together.

He continued to inspect the odd, misshaped gloves. Russell fingered the edges and his eyes brightened when he saw the hidden pairs strategically tucked inside each pair. The gloves looked dreadful, but no one would guess what she did.

"I had a feeling you'd be wanting to give some away."

"Oh Rosa, you're beautiful. You are the most genial, kind, and considerate woman."

Dr. White approached, and she moved aside while he examined Russell's leg. "I don't feel a break."

He turned to Rosa. "Just wrap it and give him a crutch since he can't walk on it. It's probably a bad sprain."

"Yes, Doctor."

"Anyone else need immediate attending to?"

"No, sir."

"Then, I'm going home." He headed toward the door and abruptly turned to her. "Have a happy Christmas, Rosa. And thank you for staying today."

"Happy Christmas to you and your family."

Russell watched the doctor leave the facility. "I like him. He's a good man."

"Yes, he is."

She bound his leg and gave him a rickety, broken crutch. They reached the door and stopped.

"Rosa."

"Yes, Russell?"

"I have another gift for you."

"Oh?"

He gently touched her chin and kissed her chastely on the lips.

"My sweet, Rosa. Your lips taste as sweet as pie."

She opened the door and watched him limp away. The gloves were clasped tightly in his hands.

The heat from Russell's tender touch raced through her. She walked away toward the infirmary. Rosa raised her shaking hands to her tingling lips, and grinned with the anticipation of future delights.

How could an innocent, chaste kiss ignite such a fiery passion in her? Heavens! Her heart was racing and her face heated.

She wanted him to kiss her again.

***

Russell had a hard time walking but managed to elude the Regulators. He was at the Negro camp and had brought them the needed medication he was stowing for them.

He needed to reach his shebang undetected. Unfortunately, he was told some pretty disheartening stories. It was much worse before he arrived at the prison.

The Raiders were fighting and stealing from the prisoners. Rumors flew among the pens; they

20

murdered fellow Union soldiers. Regulators assigned by the Confederate officers were given authority to hunt down and punish the Raiders as they deemed fit for the crimes.

There was a handful who were hanged.

It slowed them down, but it didn't stop the dishonest men. A few problem groups still fought for supplies, and stole from those who couldn't defend themselves.

When a soldier died, it was shameful the way the prisoners fought over the pathetic property left behind by the deceased.

It disgusted him thinking about it. Only the strongest survived. There was a ruthlessness among many prisoners. With hundreds of new arrivals a day, it only got worse.

And hundreds a day died from starvation and disease…some committed suicide.

The sad part was, he understood. They had become animals. Had he?

Self-preservation reigned. If they wanted to live, they had to do whatever it took. Gangs became the norm. The small group he was with supported and defended each other.

There was an intricately involved hierarchy. If he hadn't known how to fight, he'd have been fodder. His group wouldn't have shebangs or clothes. They'd be sleeping out in the camp unprotected.

What did the new prisoners think of the walking skeletons before them?

The horrifying conditions were suffocating.

This earthly oubliette should never be someone's final destination. The worm-filled hard tack, the moldy bread, the rancid meat, and the toxic water left a man wanting to die. To some, taking the chance to escape was worth the attempt. Even when they knew it was certain death.

Close to the deadline, he leaned against a rotting tree trunk, hiding from the Union guard assigned as a Regulator to protect the prisoners from the dishonest scumbags.

Russell didn't want to get caught by them either. His gaze darted to the pigeon roosts. The guards were eagle-eyed. Anyone crossing or touching the deadline would be shot and killed without warning.

He was right smack in the middle of the Regulators and Raiders constantly butting heads with each other. The enemy within, and no one to trust.

It'd gotten plum nasty.

Ten feet from his shebang someone grabbed his ankle. All he heard was the hateful curses as they beat him senseless.

***

Spring was unusually hot and humid. The incessant flies were buzzing louder than ever. Rosa's nerves were on edge, and she was about to snap at anyone who breathed wrong.

Russell was carried in by a couple of prisoners and put on a bed in the corner.

She was furious. They really did a number on him this time.

His pulse was barely discernable.

She rolled him over and inspected the welts, bruises, and deep cuts on his back and sides.

After cleaning the wounds, she carefully wrapped his torso. There were a couple of broken ribs. Hopefully, they'd heal properly. The way the bruises lay across his chest it appeared they used a thick limb from a tree.

He was semi-conscious for three days.

When Russell awoke, she blasted him, "I don't expect you to be a lickspittle, but I certainly don't want you to be a dratted idiot either."

"Why, Rosa…"

"Don't you *why Rosa* me! I've had it with this war, and anything and everything that has to do with it. I'm tired of mending you and having you come right back, worse than before.

"I'm done with hearing gunshots, knowing another man is being killed trying to cross the deadline. It's bad enough, and completely infuriating seeing them emaciated from disease and starvation."

Her eyes started pouring tears. "I'm sick of boys calling for their mothers or fathers while dying in my arms. I'm tired of the anger and hate." She burst out crying. "I'm just t-tired of it all."

"Aw, my sweet Rosa."

She cried on his shoulder, still aware of the pain he was in but needed to release all the pent-up anger, tears, and frustration.

"I love you, Russ." Tears dripped down her cheeks. "Please don't die on me."

"I'll try my best." He grinned and kissed her forehead.

They jumped when they heard a door slam.

"I'm so sorry." Rosa stood and straightened her uniform. "What was I thinking?"

Her eyes flickered to the young man next to Russell. He shrugged and smiled at her.

Turning toward the open room, she saw the same reaction from the rest of the patients. Their murmuring hushed tones quieted her distress.

She wasn't alone in her struggle to stay out of the bowels of despair. She too was a victim of circumstance.

They *all* understood.

A week later, Russell spent the night in the infirmary again. She released him a few days ago only to have him return injured and bleeding.

She walked Russell to the door of the infirmary after handing him a jar of herbal medicine. It had poured for two days and finally slowed to a drizzle. Everything was soggy and wet.

The flies were temporarily muzzled. The mosquitoes weren't. When she opened the door, they were swarmed by the biting insects.

The distant choruses and the stuttering trills from the frogs in the distance drew a line of bumps up her arms.

"Quit starting fights. I don't want to see you back here. Do you hear me?"

Russell smiled and winked. "I love you, too."

There was a loud ringing from the cast iron bell at Camp Sumter. The area inside the pens buzzed with excitement.

Dr. White came out of his office and stood next to Russell and Rosa.

A soldier approached on horseback yelling, "The war is over! The war is over!"

The doctor turned to Russell and pointed to the infirmary. "Go back to your cot."

Five officers entered the infirmary and went into the doctor's office. Rosa eyed Russell sitting on the bed and followed Dr. White.

Rosa sat in the corner and attempted to be as inconspicuous as possible. She didn't want them making her leave the room.

She wanted to hear the news!

One of the colonels read the announcement. "General Lee surrendered his troops to General Grant of the Union army at Appomattox, in Virginia.

"All prisoners of war are to be released immediately. Those infirmed are to be treated accordingly and released."

We lost.

She choked back the tears.

Bless all the souls. *It's over!*

25

Rosa had mixed emotions. She was devastated and euphoric.

They lost.

No more fighting. No more useless deaths.

Russell would be leaving her.

She didn't want him to go.

What would become of the South? It wasn't just about state's rights. It was about the rich keeping their money.

Her family never owned slaves. She didn't recall them having money problems, but she imagined her parents probably kept the worries away from the children.

She silently snorted. Not many people owned slaves. It was a very small percentage of Southerners. Only the rich could afford them, not everyday people like her family and friends.

This war couldn't have been just about slavery. That'd be a mockery of everything moral and ethical.

Why did she have the sinking feeling life was about to drastically change?

Now what would happen to them all?

What would happen to the Negroes? What would they do?

Her heart started jumping.

Such a mixture of emotions circled her heart; sadness, shock, relief, and happiness all at once.

A lone, silent tear escaped from the corner of her eye.

Elation burst through her soul. The explosion of relief and happiness filled the air with a giddiness of liberation. She was free. They were *all* free!

It was over.

Numb, Rosa watched the officers leave the office. She nodded to the doctor and the rest of the staff silently left the room. They stood around outside the office stunned at the news. No one spoke a word. They were confused, a curious mix of contrast and conviction.

Dr. White came out of his office. "Let's go. We have to decide who can be released."

Everything happened fast. Within a few days, almost all the prisoners were released and the pens were empty. A few men were in the infirmary, still unable to be moved from their beds.

Russ helped her with the care of the men who were left. He had a hard time moving about but managed to do what he could.

A few didn't make it. However, they died knowing they won the war. It was little cause for celebration when they couldn't go home to their families.

After some time, all the men were gone, leaving her with nothing to do but clean and pack everything up.

With encouragement from Rosa, Russell mustered out of the service and stayed in Georgia.

She smiled. It wasn't hard to convince him.

She wanted to continue attending to his needs. He may have told her he was fine, but she knew better. It'd take a while for the ribs to heal.

He didn't have family to go home to, nor a place to live. They were all taken from him during the long war.

She put him in the back of her wagon to bring him home.

"What will your parents think? Bringing home a Union soldier?"

"They won't be the least bit surprised. I've talked about you for months."

He grinned. "You have? Well, I'll be a monkey's uncle."

"I sent a messenger to let them know you're coming with me. I think they'll be happy to meet you."

He grunted.

Rosa laughed and gave a wide smile. "Honest. Just you wait and see. You'll be fit as a fiddle and my mum will fatten you up as fast as she can."

"You never did tell me how much I weighed. You always changed the subject."

"Do you really need to know?"

"Yes."

"Last time I weighed you, you were all of ninety pounds."

"Ninety pounds…I weighed one hundred sixty when I joined the war."

***

With open arms, Rosa's family accepted Russell into their family.

Her mother loved getting him riled up. He got snippy while he recovered. Her mother snapped at him and called him an Irishman with not a lick of sense.

Russ would turn beet red and snap, "I'm a Scot. My last name is McNamara."

Rosa laughed when she started calling him Mick and then switched to Mac. It was playful banter, and he pretended it got his goat every time.

Her mother would pipe in, "Well, bless your heart, Mac. Good thing my daughter has sense enough not to marry an Irishman!"

"I'm *not* an Irishman."

She patted his hand. "That's what I just said."

Rosa would blush. They loved each other, but he hadn't asked for her hand.

***

It was a beautiful summer day. They took some time off from their daily chores and were having a picnic.

She watched a scalawag ride by with a large wagon, and frowned. Chills ran up her arms. An unpleasant reminder of what was happening in the south.

Russ touched her arm. "You've no need to worry about them. I'm here and I'll always protect you and your family."

"I've heard some pretty bad rumors about the carpetbaggers."

"They're not taking your land. And they're not taking what's mine either."

She offered him a sad smile.

He touched her chin. "We've got something much more important to discuss."

"Oh?"

"I love you."

"I love you, too."

He held her close to his heart. She always felt safe in Russell's arms.

"What is it? Your face is flushed."

He laughed. "I'm a bit nervous, lass."

"Goodness, why?"

"Well." He paused, opened the basket, and pulled out a wrapped box. "I don't have much to offer you. But, I promise to love you forever—to be honest, hard-working, and never let you have regrets…"

"Regrets? What is it?"

"To be honest, your mother gave it to me when I asked if I could have their blessing."

"Their blessing?" She teased, watching the animated excitement dance in his eyes.

"Open it, my Rosa."

She grinned. "Did my mother wrap this for you?"

"That she did."

Rosa slowly opened the gift. Atop a silk cloth lay her grandmother's sapphire and diamond ring.

"Will you marry me?" He took the ring and put it on her finger. "A simple, broken man who fought for the other side? A man with a permanent limp, and scars all over his body and soul?"

"You, my love, will never be a simple man. You're a hero to me, and to many of the men at Andersonville."

"No, I'm no hero. I just did what needed to be done."

"You went above and beyond. You didn't need to help those men get medical supplies. You could've looked the other way, but instead, you fought for them. Helped them live and survive."

"You're making me out to be braver than I am."

Rosa touched his scarred cheek. "No, I'm not. You could have stayed in your shebang, licked your wounds, and ignored everything around you. But *my* Russell wouldn't sit around and let anyone suffer needlessly…and it's one of the biggest reasons why I love you."

"So does that mean yes?"

She offered a merry laugh. "Yes, I will marry you."

He kissed her, slowly and passionately. Desire warmed Rosa's heart. Her soul hummed, and she reveled in the feel of his touch.

Russell admired the ring on her finger, before looking into her eyes. "I knew it the day I met you."

"Oh?"

"Yes, I told you. *A Rosa for Russell.*"

Two Step, New Steps

by

Debra Parmley

Two Step, New Step

Bartlett Police Officer Leonard "Len" Yardley was less than thrilled to be on desk duty while his arm and shoulder healed from a gunshot wound he'd received a week ago. But that was the rule of the precinct and doctor's orders. So, Len was stuck inside at a desk filling out paperwork. It hadn't put him in the best of moods.

Civilians had no idea how much paperwork cops did, even the cops out in patrol cars. Paperwork was his least favorite thing about his job. He liked having his feet on the ground, meeting challenges head on and moving forward into them. That was his way. To be out among the people, or driving the streets and keeping them safe. Not stuck inside an office all day.

He was restless, but looking forward to attending a cookout next Saturday at Nash Ware's place. Nash was planning to ask his girlfriend to marry him and if she said yes, the barbeque would be a celebration of their engagement.

Nash's girl, Betsy Bobbin, was a quiet librarian who worked at the Bartlett Library. Nash was clearly head over heels in love with her. True love was good to see. Too often Len saw the other side of people. He needed the reminder that some marriages were good ones and actually meant to last.

***

Len opted to wear a loose Hawaiian print shirt which

covered his bandage. No one would know he was hurt unless he told them.

Leaving his Harley in the garage, he drove his truck to Nash's house and parked down the street.

The street was already lined with cars. Nash's driveway and the drive next door were full, so Len parked one street over. Other than the nine-millimeter Len always carried, along with his spare pistol and his I.D., which wouldn't come out unless it was necessary, nothing marked him as a cop.

He walked toward Nash's house, taking in the other houses and checking Nash's out.

Len had met the Marine veteran with the eye patch at the local Harley dealership fundraiser ride for the children's hospital last month.

Nash had an unusual set up, on account of having sight in only one eye. He had a series of custom mirrors mounted on his bike to give him good visibility and he rode a 2003 Harley Road King, one hundredth anniversary special, that he'd restored after he came home from the Middle East.

He also preferred to ride with at least one other biker, so for the children's fundraising ride, they'd paired up. Len had enjoyed getting to know the quiet Marine vet. He was, as Len's grandfather would have said, "a solid guy." They'd stayed in touch, and Len had been invited to the barbeque.

Walking to the backyard fence, he pushed the door open and looked for Nash. Spotting the Marine over by the barbeque grill, Len stepped out and walked over to him. "Hey, Nash, great day for a barbeque."

"It is," Nash shook his hand and then glanced up

at the sky using his good eye to get a good look. He grinned. "Not one rain cloud in sight."

Last week they'd had rain every single day. Sunshine and blue clouds were a welcome sight.

The back door opened and a pretty woman with long blonde hair and blue eyes stepped out carrying an oven mitt. "Betsy sent this out for you and said Pete's running late. He's bringing more ice and a big tub of vanilla ice cream."

Nash grinned. "This party just gets better and better. Leann, I'd like you to meet Officer Len Yardley."

So much for no one knowing he was a cop. But that didn't matter now.

"Hello," Len said, smiling down at the prettiest girl there. With her beautiful smile, nice curves and a glow which went beyond her lightly tanned skin, she could have stepped out of his dreams. He wanted to get to know her.

"Hello," she said, smiling up at him. "It's nice to meet you, Officer Yardley."

"You can call me Len."

"Len, I'm glad you could come to the celebration," she said. "This is a big day for my sister, Betsy. And for Nash."

She was clearly happy for her sister. She almost bubbled over with genuine excitement. It shone in her eyes and across her face. Rosy cheeks and bright blue eyes looked back at him.

He couldn't help but smile deeper.

"Officer Yardley is with the Bartlett Police Department," Nash said.

"Ooh a policeman," Leann looked up at Len with new admiration. "I love policemen."

Len smiled at her and wondered why she looked familiar. Maybe it was her resemblance to her sister Betsy.

"How long have you been a policeman?"

"I wanted to be a cop ever since I was a little kid, so the minute I graduated from Bartlett High School, I signed up to be a military cop with the Air Force. Served six years in security forces and made sergeant before coming home to join the Bartlett Police Department. I've been there two years," he said.

"Oh wow. So, are you one of the men who came to the mall after that stalker tried to abduct me?"

His face went serious. "No, I wasn't there. You had a stalker?"

"It's a long story," she shrugged. "I'd bore you."

"This party just started," he said. "We have plenty of time and no, you won't bore me. Tell me."

"This was two years ago. That's why I thought you were one of the policemen who was there."

"I would've been newly hired and likely writing traffic tickets. Everyone starts out that way. So, what happened?"

Leann's sister Betsy, the librarian, came out the back door of the house, carrying a bowl of coleslaw and two big packages of buns. She placed them on the long table just beyond the barbeque grill. "I thought I bought four packages of buns but they weren't in the grocery bags. So, I called Jim. He's picking up two more on his way," she said.

"That's great, honey," Nash said. "And Lance is

bringing some kind of vegetarian dish because his new girlfriend doesn't eat meat."

"I'm glad they're bringing something she can eat," she said, her eyes wide. "I didn't think about anyone being vegetarian. All three of your buddies will be late. I guess we'd better let everyone start eating and not wait on them."

"Betsy, stop fussing. Come and meet Len," Leann said.

Betsy walked up to them, and they were introduced.

Len had seen Betsy and knew of the pretty librarian but hadn't met her.

She has a sweet motherly nature. No wonder the children of Bartlett love story hour at the library with Miss Betsy.

"Everything is ready, so dig in," Betsy said, but her soft voice didn't carry enough to be heard.

Nash told everyone, louder, in his Marine voice.

Len grinned. Marines and cops learned how to use a commanding voice people heard immediately. He could see Nash commanding troops.

Party goers lined up and began filling their plates.

Len got in line behind Leann and hoped they'd continue their conversation after they went through the line.

When each had a plate full of food he said, "Where do you want to sit?"

"Over by the bird feeder," she said.

He glanced around the yard but didn't see one.

"The black pedestal with the lamp on top," Leann said.

Then he realized the lamp was a bird feeder open on each side instead of having glass panels.

"Nash likes to tinker with things taking other things out of them," Leann said. "He's very creative."

"Clever idea."

They headed to two seats nearby and sat by a small table. The cozy arrangement might help her share her story.

After they were seated, he said, "You were telling me what happened with your stalker."

"I was in college at Eastern Kentucky and had two more years to finish my degree in marketing. There was a guy in my algebra class who developed a crush on me. He signed up to be my tutor and tried to get close, but he wasn't my type, so I didn't let him."

His eyebrow went up. "Someone in your class signed up to be your tutor?"

"Yeah, that didn't raise a red flag for me at the time," she admitted. "My sister pointed that out later. He seemed to think I was his girlfriend even though I kept turning him down for dates. He was always texting me or messaging me on social media. It was like he watched every single thing I did. I needed to keep going to tutoring because I suck at algebra and I needed to pass."

"You couldn't find another tutor?"

"Well, I didn't think of it," she admitted. "Then I came to Bartlett to visit my sister, Betsy, and he messaged me about my kitten, Mr. Whiskers."

Len smiled at the name and then forced the smile away to be serious again as he listened.

"He kidnapped Mr. Whiskers on campus. But I was afraid to talk to him even though I knew he had Mr. Whiskers. He really creeped me out. A *lot*."

"You had a good reason to be creeped out," Len said. "A pattern of abusing animals is a red flag for criminal behavior. Always trust your gut feeling."

"He turned out to be even crazier. After those texts, he came to Bartlett with my kitten. He wanted me to get into his van to get my fur baby. I wanted to rescue Mr. Whiskers."

"I yelled at her not to do it," Betsy had walked over as they spoke. "We'd just come out of the Wolfchase Galleria Mall, and he'd parked his white van right next to my car. He was waiting inside, ready to entice her with her kitten in a cage."

"I just wanted Mr. Whiskers," Leann said. "I didn't know he had a knife."

"Never get in the vehicle. For any reason," Len said. "Do everything you can to stay out of it, scream, shout, fight."

"I wasn't going to get in," she shook her head. "I knew to listen to Betsy. But he had a knife. And he grabbed me."

"I'd called Nash, and he was on his way," Betsy said. "Thank God. It was terrifying."

"When Malcom grabbed me and tried to pull me into the van, Nash pulled up in his truck and went for him. He saved my life."

"Malcom," Len said. "Would that be Malcom Hess?"

"Yes, that's him," Leann nodded.

"I recall hearing about him after they hired me. He had a prior history of stalking. He never made it to trial and died in the hospital."

"They took him away in an ambulance. He had

broken ribs and a punctured lung. That killed him before they could save him. I was so glad. He'd terrorized me for months. Now I'll never have to see him again. And I was so glad I had Mr. Whiskers back."

"I'm glad too. And how is Mr. Whiskers today?"

"He's not a kitten any more, but he's still a noisy night owl, and he gets into everything. He's been very naughty this month. Between finals and graduation, I haven't been home much."

"Graduation?"

"Leann just graduated from the University of Memphis with a BA in marketing," Betsy said, clearly proud of her sister.

"Congratulations," he smiled at Leann.

"Thank you," she said, smiling back.

"What's next?" he asked.

"I start working at Southern Security Bank," she said. "Assistant manager of the Bartlett branch."

"Nice," he said.

"Yes," she nodded. "It's the most adult job I've ever had. Lots of responsibility."

"If they didn't think you were up to it, they wouldn't have hired you."

"True, I suppose." She nodded.

"No supposing. Bankers are dry and careful people," he said. "They're careful not to make mistakes."

"I wore my sister's most conservative suit to the interview," she said. "I think that helped."

"I'm sure it did," he said.

"Two years ago, Leann was in her sorority party girl phase," Betsy said. "Picture bleach blonde hair, black leather skirt and black leather boots."

"Nothing wrong with leather," Len said. He didn't mention his Harley. Today he'd driven the truck.

Leann in leather. She'd be hot.

"Your natural color looks better than that white blonde," Betsy said to Leann. "It goes with your skin tone. I'm sure the conservative look helped you get the bank job."

"I think so too." Leann nodded. "They even have a dress code! I didn't know anyone still did that!"

"A college campus isn't the real world," Betsy said. "I can't imagine going to class in pajamas. I don't even run to the drugstore for a prescription dressed like that when I'm sick."

Leann laughed. "No, you wouldn't. I've been to classes at EKU and to get ice cream in mine."

"Ice cream?" Betsy's eyes widened, and she shook her head.

Len quietly laughed. The two sisters were very different. He wasn't about to tell them he didn't own a pair of pajamas. He threw on exercise shorts and carried his gun if he went to answer his front door. Most nights he slept commando.

"Back then I never worried about anything, least of all what someone thought about what I was wearing. These days I'm looking for more security in my life." Leann had turned serious. "Hey, speaking of security, when is the big announcement?"

"Right after everyone eats their barbeque and before the cake comes out. We even have an engagement cake!" Betsy said.

"If it's supposed to be a secret, you're not keeping

it very well." Leann laughed. "You might want to whisper."

"Whispering makes people listen closer, and a whisper can carry," Len dropped his voice low. "For a secret, it's better to lower your voice, like this."

Leann, leaning in to hear him better, breathed in, catching his scent.

His cologne is nice. His smile is even nicer. And his muscles? The nicest of all.

She didn't mind getting closer to him. Being near him raised her senses to a level she hadn't reached with anyone. Even the colors around them seemed brighter. It had to be pheromones, and his sexy voice did a number on her inside.

I wish he'd talk to me more in that low, sexy voice.

"I wonder what kind of cake it is," she murmured, her voice now low too.

"Carrot cake with cream cheese icing," Betsy said. "I went with Nash's favorite. But he doesn't know."

"Sounds delicious," Len said.

"What's your favorite cake?" Leann asked Len.

"Red Velvet," he said.

"Oh, that's a good one," Leann said. "I've never made one of those. Just strawberry or chocolate. Betsy is the baker."

"Do you cook?" he asked Leann.

"Oh yeah. That's my chili dip over there. I've got a big pot of chili at home. Always make a lot when I take my chili dip somewhere. I end up freezing it because it's more than Betsy and I can eat."

"I'll have to try your dip," he said. "Sounds good." He made a point of getting up to go help himself to her dip and corn chips to dip into it.

Betsy watched him go. "Kind of old for you, isn't he?"

Leann frowned. "No. And anyway, we're just talking."

"Right. That's why you're leaning in, showing off your cleavage. Just take it slow, please, and be careful."

"Betsy, he's a *cop*. You don't find a safer guy to date than a cop. And if he's older, so what? I *like* him. And besides he hasn't asked me out. We just met."

"Oh, he's interested. Please go slow. You just broke up with Stanford."

"Yeah, well, Stanford is an ass. A wealthy one, but still an ass. Officer Yardley is nothing like Stanford."

Stanford Westland the third. God's gift to women. Or so he thinks. He has impeccable manners, high standards, and he was charming at first. God only knows what makes him criticize everything about me now, when he supposedly liked me so much in the beginning.

Len came back with food on his plate and a large helping of her dip. He sat down. "Your dip is good. I snuck a bite."

"Testing it before you loaded up?" she laughed. "Making sure I wouldn't poison you."

He laughed. "No poisoning allowed. My coworkers would be all over you."

"I guess that's true!" she laughed.

Oh good. Not only is he a sexy cop, he has a good sense of humor, too.

"I'm glad you like my dip," she said. "My ex-boyfriend has been telling me for months I don't make it right. Apparently, I don't cook anything right."

"He's an idiot," Len said, "Look at all the people going back for seconds." He pointed his thumb over toward the table and took another scoop of his own.

"Well, how about that," she said. "They sure are."

Knowing that gave her great satisfaction.

Yes, Stanford is an idiot. Everyone has always said my dip is delicious. Except him.

"I wouldn't be surprised if everything you cook is good," Len said.

"My sister says I fix dishes just like mama did."

"Then there you go." Len nodded.

She beamed. Being with him made her heart happy. Even if he was older than she was, she liked him and was going to follow her heart.

"I'm really glad we met," she said.

"I'm glad too." He smiled back. "I'd like to learn more about you."

"What would you like to know?"

"What are your hobbies?"

"I love to go dancing, though it's been a while because I've been busy with school, job hunting and apartment hunting. I live with my sister, but I'm moving into a new place next week."

"Where are you moving?"

"I'll still be in Bartlett; I just can't keep living with my sister. It's time I was on my own, in my own apartment with no roommates."

"Just you and Mr. Whiskers?"

"That's right." She nodded. "I was in a sorority house in Kentucky, but then after my stalker, I moved in with Betsy and transferred to the University of Memphis. I didn't want to live away from family after what happened."

"I can see that."

"But I'm over it." She shrugged. "Ready to move on."

"Sounds like you're well on your way."

"I don't start at the Bartlett branch for another week and I'm in bank training at the main branch first," she said. "I might catch a matinee next week. Would you like to go?"

"I'd love to, but I'm on day shift, so it couldn't be a matinee. What about dinner and a movie?"

Oh, he's asking me on a date. Dinner and a movie. Yes. That's definitely a date. Oh good.

"Yes, I'd *love* that. I don't even know what's on. I was just excited about making a matinee for a change. It's been a while since I saw a movie. Yes, dinner and a movie sound awesome. I'd love to go with you."

Oh no. Do I sound too enthusiastic? Stanford always said I needed to tone it down and not seem so excited all the time. Maybe he's right.

"Wednesday night?"

"Yes, that's perfect," she said.

"It's a date."

"Yes," she smiled as happiness bubbled up within.

A date! It's a date. With Len. Who's sexy as sin. I can't help but grin. Oh no. I've been living with Betsy and her books too long, and now I'm starting to sing-song rhyme like her.

"Betsy, come here, I have a surprise for you," Nash called.

She moved over next to him.

He put his hands over her eyes. "No peeking now."

"This is going to be good," Leann whispered to

Len. "I know what her surprise is."

"Ready," Nash said. "Bring on the surprise."

A woman who resembled Betsy and Leann but with long brown hair, entered through the backyard gate, wearing a large camera around her neck and a huge smile.

Leann clapped her hands together. "I can't wait to see the look on Betsy's face."

Nash removed his hands and said, "Surprise!"

Betsy's eyes widened and her face lifted with joy. "Virginia! I can't believe you're here!"

"Of course!" Virginia said. "I wouldn't miss this!"

The two women embraced.

"That's our oldest sister, Virginia," Leann giggled. "She's a wedding photographer and flew in to join us and to take engagement pictures."

"What a great surprise," Len said. "Sisters reunited. How long has it been since you've seen her?"

"Yesterday." Leann laughed. "I picked her up at the airport and took her to a hotel where Betsy wouldn't see her. We had lunch and got caught up. Look at Betsy, she's glowing with happiness."

"She is," Len agreed.

"Attention everyone," Nash said, his Marine voice booming out over the crowd which filled the backyard. They all gave him their attention.

Virginia moved back, getting her camera ready.

"I'd like to announce that this lovely woman by my side, Miss Betsy Marie Bobbin, has agreed to marry me." He reached for her hand and held it high so everyone could see the engagement ring she now wore. "We've set the date for next year, in June. Tonight, we're celebrating our engagement!"

"Congratulations!" Guests yelled and clapped.

"Hoorah!" Nash's Marine buddies yelled. One came up and clapped him once on the back.

A crowd gathered around the happy couple.

Leann clasped her hands together, joyful tears in her eyes.

"Looks like true love," Len said.

"Oh, it is," she whispered, blinking.

"It does exist," he said.

"I believe it does," she said, then whispered, "I believe."

***

Seeing Leann's true emotions clearly on display, Len knew she was wearing her heart on her sleeve. Her sweet, innocent, trusting heart made her even more beautiful.

He was falling fast, yet he barely knew her. Within her family circle, she was fully herself, and he liked what he saw.

Stanford really is an idiot. Sucks to be him. He's missing out. But all the better for me.

Miss Leann Bobbin had a heart wish for true love with an ex-boyfriend who was critical and didn't appreciate her, a new apartment, a new job, and a wish for a new and better future.

Ready to be a part of her future, if things worked out, Len realized he hadn't told her about his injury.

Could she handle dating a cop? Could she live with the fact that one night her boyfriend might never come home?

At some point we'll need to talk about that. But we haven't even gone on our first date yet. I'm already wounded, and she doesn't know. It's too soon to tell her. I don't want anything to take away from the joy on her face right now.

He remained silent.

We'll get to that. Later.

For now, he'd enjoy his time with her. She was a breath of fresh air. Being around her lightened him considerably.

"I'll get us some cake," she said. "Big piece or little?"

"Big," he said and winked.

She giggled and hurried into the crowd.

Even her giggle is adorable. She doesn't seem old enough to be a college graduate and a bank manager.

Her sweet girlish innocence was a large part of her attraction, though he believed she'd be even more beautiful as she got older. Tonight, her bubbly nature made him want to laugh out loud. She was as intoxicating as the champagne bubbles in the glasses they were now passing around.

***

The next morning at breakfast Betsy asked, "Did you have fun at the party last night?"

"I did," Leann said. "It was great."

"Thanks." Betsy cleared her throat. "So, Officer

Yardley, the older guy you were talking to all night, don't you think he's too old for you?"

"You make him sound like an old man. He's only twenty-seven. That's just four years older."

"He seems a lot older."

"He's just serious because he has a serious job," Leann said. "It makes him appear older than he is."

"Maybe so," Betsy said. "But be careful. You should focus on your new job and apartment. Moving day is Tuesday. Nash says he'll help, and I have the day off. Oh, and I'm giving you Mom's rocking chair so you'll have something from back home."

"Thanks sis." Leann smiled. "Love you."

"I love you, too." Betsy came over to give her a hug.

Leann's cat, Mr. Whiskers, wove himself around Leann's ankles in a figure eight, something he did when her attention was occupied elsewhere. He always got her attention that way.

She had no idea what crazy Malcomb Hess had done to Mr. Whiskers while he'd had him, beyond not feeding him, and didn't want to imagine. She didn't want to think about him ever again. Though Mr. Whiskers seemed fine after she got him back, he still shied away from men, not letting them hold him or stroke him.

She picked him up, walked to her mother's rocking chair and sat down. Rocking him had become a comfort for them both after their ordeal. Leann closed her eyes and rocked.

It's so quiet.

After Nash and Betsy left, Leann stood inside her new apartment, surrounded by boxes they'd just carried in the room. She now had the apartment to herself, was living alone for the first time in her life. She was glad and feeling independent.

Mr. Whiskers wove a figure eight around her ankles again.

She pulled him close to her chest and stroked the fluffy cat who'd been at the pet grooming salon while the move was underway. He'd need plenty of petting after she'd subjected him to the groomers and being moved from one home to another, all in one day. She didn't want him sulking.

"Well, Mr. Whiskers. What do you think of our new home?"

The cat didn't meow, but pushed his head under her hand for more stroking in the spot he wanted. She indulged him and moved over to the rocker to sit and rock with him.

Looking around as she sat, she eyed her cream colored, neutral apartment. "I don't own much," she said, taking in the empty room and stacks of boxes. "But, this apartment needs some color before I have guests."

Standing and putting Mr. Whiskers down, she moved over to one of the boxes and opened it. Inside was a small bookcase that she'd have to reassemble before filling it with her books. She needed a new one.

She had more books than would fit and the legs and shelves had become loose and wobbly after going from sorority house to Betsy's house to her apartment. It was cheap and not meant to hold up move after move.

She put the bookcase together, and gave it a small nudge. It wobbled way too much. Taking out a notepad and pen, she jotted down:

Bigger book shelves

Book ends

Colorful Flower vase

Food

Cat food

Colorful pillows

There was a lot she'd do once she started getting paid. The new job was days away, and she couldn't wait.

The phone rang, and she answered it.

"How's the new apartment?" Len asked.

"It's great," she said. "I moved in an hour ago." She laughed. "You're my first caller."

"I'd like to be your first visitor. Can I drop by? I picked up a little something for you," he said.

"Sure, just don't expect much. It's mostly boxes. I can find the glasses before you get here though."

"Hey, I don't expect to be entertained," he said. "I just want to see you."

"I want to see you, too."

"I'm pulling in right now."

"That was fast."

"Almost there."

She heard him head up the steps, and she hurried to look out. Before he knocked, she opened the door. "Hello."

"Hello," he smiled and then from behind his back brought out a small bouquet of flowers in a clear vase. "I thought these might brighten up your new place."

"Oh, they're beautiful," she said. "Thank you." She took the flowers and gave him a great big smile. "They're perfect. Welcome to my new home. Come on in."

He stepped inside and looked at the wobbly bookcase.

"I need to get a new one after I get paid," she said. "It's on the list."

"Let me look at it," he said and went over to it, while she placed the flowers on the kitchen island which separated the small kitchen from the living room.

"A few screws would hold it together for now." He squatted down to look at the bookshelves closer. "But it's not solid wood, and it's gotten damp at some point."

"It's been in my sister's garage," she said. "I didn't move all my stuff in when I moved there."

"Do you have a screwdriver?" he asked.

"No," she shook her head. I don't have any tools,"

"I'll bring mine and come pick you up for dinner," he said.

"That sounds great. Thank you."

***

The music at The Electric Cowboy had Leann tapping her toes.

Len watched her foot for a moment and then

grinned and held out his hand. "Ready to dance?"

"More than ready." She placed her hand in his. "It's been too long."

"Then let's go."

On the dance floor as the music changed, he led her into the Texas two-step.

Two step, new steps, she thought. *My life has finally changed since the last time I was here.*

She no longer downed margaritas to escape the stress of being stalked. Her ex was out of the picture and her new boyfriend was a great guy. They'd been to dinner and a movie, he'd fixed her bookcase and later helped her pick out a new, solid oak bookcase.

Her new life felt perfect. Like nothing could go wrong. Len made her feel safe; in his arms it felt like home.

***

Leann loved her new job and was filing away paperwork when a noise behind her office, out in the main area of the bank, made her turn her head.

Two men, wearing black hooded sweatshirts, ran into the bank, holding guns out in front of them.

"Hands up!" the one with the red tennis shoes screamed and shot his gun once into the air, hitting the ceiling tile.

"Everyone get down on the ground!" the other one yelled.

Leann, in the office, had turned toward them,

frozen in shock, where they hadn't seen her yet.

Bang.

She jumped, dropping the paperwork onto the floor as she slid around behind the filing cabinet hoping they wouldn't see her or find her.

She reached into her jacket pocket, turned her cell phone volume down, and dialed the last number who'd called her last night. Len Yardley.

It rang, and he answered.

"There's a man with a gun here," she said softly into her phone the minute he answered.

He texted back.

Stay calm baby we're coming keep your phone on.

"Okay," she whispered. "There are two of them, two guns."

Her bank training which she'd just completed had taught her to pay attention to details.

How many men? How many guns? How tall are they? What color are their eyes? Distinguishing marks or features?

She had few details, and her mind was in shock. One had red shoes. Both wore black. She had no idea how tall they were or anything else.

Red shoe man and black hood.

She nicknamed them in her head. Unable to see what was going on, she could still hear the yelling coming from the bank lobby. One of the tellers was crying.

Leann began to worry less about herself and more about her co-workers.

She leaned her head out around the corner of the filing cabinet and tried to see what was going on.

One of the robbers was pulling money from

Cassandra's cash drawer and stuffing it into a pillowcase with jerking, sharp movements.

The other was waving his gun around, alternating between turning the gun on its side and pointing from one bank teller to another. His pants were falling down in back and with his other hand he yanked them up again. He seemed twitchy, and acted strange, like he was on something.

Were the police coming?

She couldn't reach the silent alarms and hoped one of the other tellers had pressed an alarm, like they'd been trained to do. She'd called Len. He'd been the first one she'd reached out to, because she trusted him. He'd said they were coming. Where were they?

She was scared, and she wanted Len.

He'd know just what to do. She didn't.

Flashing lights outside the building let her know that at least one police car had pulled up in front.

Would the robbers go out the front doors or the back?

Please God, don't let them shoot anyone. Let them just take the money and go.

***

Len hurried into the dispatchers' room and said, "We've got a robbery in progress at Southern Security Bank. Two suspects are armed. Leann Bobbins saw them."

One dispatcher ended the call she was on and held out her hand for the phone to collect the intel. His phone was already on mute, from the moment Leann said there were men with guns.

He handed the phone over to the dispatcher and tried taking slow breaths to calm himself. He had a strong urge to run outside to his squad car right this minute and go peeling out of the parking lot, siren blazing.

The charge to the rescue gene was strong in him, but that wouldn't be the way to save her.

Time was of the essence. He talked fast. "My girlfriend was hired last week as assistant manager. She called me."

And she's scared to death.

He didn't say it out loud.

The dispatcher nodded and noted Leann's name and position in a place on her computer then called patrol cars.

"We have a 10-46 in progress at 6262 Stage Road. Suspects are armed," she said.

"Do we know anything else?" she asked Len.

"No," he said. "She went silent."

The captain came into the room. "What's going on, Len?"

"That's my girl, captain. She called me," he said.

"Instead of 9-1-1?"

"Yes." He nodded. "She's only been on the job a week."

"Her position?"

"Assistant manager."

"Is the manager there?"

"I don't know."

They both knew the senior bank personnel on site could quickly become a target.

Calls were coming in to the other dispatcher about gunshots fired in the vicinity. The most recent caller was saying two men wearing hoods had entered the bank, carrying guns.

Len frowned and focused on listening.

Two armed men. Leann, I need to hear you. Speak to me.

There was no other sound he wanted to hear more than her voice right now, to know she was alive and okay.

There'd been no further communication from her. The only sounds coming from her phone were of the bank robbers screaming at the employees. The dispatcher manning his phone had hooked it up to headphones and was listening close. But now Len couldn't hear what was happening, and it was driving him crazy.

It took everything Len had within himself not to charge to the rescue. His good gun arm was still healing, and he was emotionally involved with a possible hostage.

Every logical reason said *no, you can't go.*

Every other part of him screamed *the hell I can't, I'm going to protect my woman.*

The problem was, racing to protect her could be what endangered her more.

He'd begun pacing and cracking his knuckles, behavior he was barely aware of.

"You're not yourself right now, Len," his captain said. "But you're doing the right thing."

"Not myself," he shook his head as he paced. "I need to be there. That's my girl."

"I know, and that's damn hard."

"It's not my nature to stand down," Len growled. "And sure as hell not when it's my woman in danger."

"I'll let you ride with me; with the understanding you'll stay in the patrol car until I give the okay. Understand?"

"Yes," Len growled again. The only word he could get out through gritted teeth.

***

Police cars converged on the bank encircling it and keeping all bystanders away, far from the bank and the gunmen. They were there as much to protect the people outside of the bank as the people within.

It didn't stop the curious from hovering on the outer fringe of that circle, trying to see what was going on.

The SWAT team was out in full force and ready to move in or to fire from their positions.

"Hold. One man coming out with a hostage."

Len gripped the door handle, his knuckles white as he listened.

Don't let it be Leann.

But it was.

Her long blonde hair and curvy shape were unmistakable even from a distance.

Len opened the squad car door and stepped out.

"Stand down," the captain said to him.

Len couldn't answer or move, every bit of tension wired taut as he listened and watched Leann being forced to walk in front of the bank robber.

"Don't nobody move, or I shoot her!" a black man wearing a black hood, black pants and red tennis shoes shouted and jerked her in front of him, using her as a shield, and waved his gun screaming, "Move, you stupid bitch!"

Then Leann did something that surprised Len.

She let her weight go heavy and dropped flat onto the ground, pulling the robbers arm with her.

Good girl.

The move was just enough to bring her body away from the robber, no longer a shield and now SWAT team could take shots.

Bang.

Bang.

First shot hit the first bank robber.

He screamed and started shooting wildly.

A volley of shots from the SWAT team followed.

Leann stayed flat on the ground, her hands over her head, protecting it as she screamed.

Both robbers were down and stayed down as police ran forward to take their guns away and check for pulses.

Len was out of the squad car and running.

The captain let him go without a word.

Leann was on the ground, her hands over her head screaming and shaking. Bullets had flown over her head, and then it was quiet.

Suddenly Len was there, his warm strong hands pulling her arms away from her head, checking her body, moving fast.

"Baby, are you hurt? Did they hit you?"

She looked into his eyes. "Len."

He was here now. Her handsome boyfriend, who'd already been shot once, who was worried about her, had come for her.

"You're here."

"Of course I'm here." Seeing she wasn't shot, he pulled her into his arms and held her close. She felt the heavy bullet proof vest beneath his shirt instead of his chest which brought home what his job was, what he did every day, possibly putting himself into the line of fire. A place she'd just been.

He'd already brought the subject up, worried she wouldn't be able to handle being with a cop long term. Not every woman could be.

But she didn't care. Danger could find them anywhere they were. It didn't matter what your job was. She could just as easily have been making a deposit into her bank account when the robbers walked in.

"I love you Len," she started to cry. "I'm so glad to be alive, and I love you."

"Oh, baby," he said. "I'm glad you're alive too, and I love you too, sweetheart." He squeezed her tighter. "I don't know what I'd have done if something happened to you."

Knowing what it felt like to fear for her life, he never wanted to be in that position again and vowed to make sure she was safe for as long as she would have him.

They were surrounded by officers now. Some marking off the outline of the two bodies with chalk, some taking pictures and the media person at the edge of the circle where citizens were kept back along with the press, ready to talk to them.

"Come on," he said. "You'll need to be checked out by the EMT's then you'll have to give your statement of what happened. But I'll be right here, and when we're done, I'm taking you home."

"All right, Len," she said. "I remember from before when I had to give a statement. I'll be all right." She stood up straight and rolled her shoulders. "Let's get started."

"You're amazing," he said. "Do you know that?"

She smiled at him. "As long as you think so."

"I know so," he took her hand and walked her over to the EMTs who were checking over a pregnant woman who was a teller at the bank.

"You okay?" Leann asked the woman.

"Yes, everything seems to be fine," she said.

"Oh good," Leann exhaled. "Guess I'm next then."

After they were done, Len drove her to his place, and they ordered a pizza with plans to stay in, take the phone off the hook and curl up to watch a movie.

He couldn't keep his hands off of her. Touching her reaffirmed she was still alive, still physically unharmed.

His hands pulled her to him and her hands roamed over him as they kissed. Hungry for each other they forgot all about the pizza, and it wasn't until the doorbell rang that they remembered.

"I'll be right back," he said. He reached for his wallet in the back pocket of his pants and went to the door to pay for the pizza.

Opening the door, he paid the delivery man and taking the pizza, he then closed the door. "Are you hungry?"

"I'm only hungry for you," she said, her hand on the bedroom door.

"Pizza can wait," he said and he went to join her.

THE END

Bringing Her Home

by

Teri Riggs

Prologue

Tommy

"We're going to die!" Jess yelled.

"Not today, darlin'!" I shouted over the noisy report of bullets flying around us. "We've got this!"

"You should break the news to the asshats shooting at us, Tommy. They obviously haven't received the memo."

We returned a steady stream of fire, taking out more traffickers. We'd been ambushed, and the rest of our team were down. I had no clue if my FBI team was dead or alive. I saw Jazz move his hand once. The other two? Not a muscle twitch or response to our shout outs. Not a good sign at all.

"Dammit, Tommy. What happened to our *simple* take down?"

"Fuck if I know." I fired a couple more rounds, wishing I had my sniper rifle. "My guess? Someone in the Bureau sold us out."

"My thoughts too," Jess said.

Nobody liked to admit people they trust would betray them. My shock at being ambushed turned to anger.

I reloaded my Sig, took aim, and fired again.

Ten more minutes ticked by. I estimated three or four men were left firing at us. At the first break in the shooting, I rushed the remaining shooters. I nailed two of them, and Jess, who'd followed, took out two.

"I'll check on our guys. You take care of these bastards," Jess said, pointing at the dead men.

"Will there be a reward for my good behavior?" I tease. "Like maybe sex?"

"Oh my God, Tommy. That's so inappropriate." She laughs and winks at me. "When we get home, that's the plan."

Yeah, inappropriate, but I wanted to see one more smile from Jess before this nightmare gets worse. Our team members are likely dead, and she'll take it hard.

I kicked one of the trafficker's boots. *Dead*. Before Jess took two steps, she turned around and gave me a thumbs up. That's when another one of the *dead* bastards rose, pointing his gun in my direction. He'd had a fucking Kevlar vest on.

Jess knocks into me, at the same time firing her weapon. She nailed the shooter's forehead, dead center. He dropped like a sack of bricks, a look of shock blanketing his face. Next to me, Jess hit the dirt.

I offered her a hand up. "Dammit, Jess, be careful. I was ready to fire when you knocked into me. I could've shot you."

She looked at me, her eyes glassy. "Couldn't take a chance, Tommy. I could never live without you."

Her voice was weak, and I couldn't pull her to her feet. "What the fuck, Jess?"

That's when I saw blood running though the fingers of the hand she held over her belly. The woman I loved more than anything in the world had been shot trying to protect me while I'd been too busy making jokes about sex to notice what was going on around me.

Chapter One

Tommy

Two years later…

I, Former FBI Agent turned CPD Bureau of Organized Crime detective, Thomas Raintree, am making slow, sweet love to my beautiful Jess. I alternated running my hand and tongue over her perfect breasts, tweaking her nipples into hard pebbles. Her heavy breathing spurred me on, making my erection harder than granite. My dick was about to explode.

"I love you, darlin'. So damned much." I walked my fingers from her breasts and down her torso until I hit the spot between her legs I was aiming for.

"Love you more," Jess moaned in between gasps.

She called my name louder as I thrust into her harder. I circle my finger over her clit. Her cries become higher-pitched, and my balls tighten. I'm moments away from reaching my peak. Her deep shrills become brassier with a steady cadence. She's almost there too, and I'd be damned if I'll climax before Jess.

I realized the twilling sound wasn't Jess in the throes of ecstasy. Nope. It's my cell phone sitting on the coffee table next to an empty pizza box. Jess's beautiful face fades and the tight grip her body had on my erection released. "Fuck." The ringing interrupted my erotic dream moments before I found relief for my aching dick. And damn did it ache.

At least I hadn't come in my boxers like a pimple-faced, sixteen-year-old. But I was damned-sure going to jump in the shower and take care of my throbbing dick.

"This better be fuckin' good," I growled into my phone.

"It is," my boss, Captain Kingsman said, voice gruff.

"Shit, Captain." I glanced around the room. I'm not in my bed, and I sure as hell am not holding Jess in my arms. I'd fallen asleep on my couch again. I sat up and ran a hand through my hair. "I didn't bother to check the caller ID." Finding the remote, I turned off the TV.

"Obviously. Wake your ass up and come into the station ASAP. We have a fuckin' problem." Kingsman disconnected.

I flipped on the end table lamp and took in a deep breath. What problem could possibly be more important than time spent with Jess in my dreams? Two years after we'd parted ways; it's the only way I could be with her. In my dreams, we're still together.

I could touch her.

Smell her.

Taste her.

When I was awake? I had nothing but bad memories. The dreams are better than the reality.

And the reality was, I haven't seen Jess since the day I'd almost gotten her killed.

"Sit, Raintree," Captain Kingsman ordered.

"Thanks." I rolled my neck from side to side, trying to work out the kinks.

"The FBI needs help finding a missing person."

I flicked a piece of lint off my tee shirt.

"Wake up and pay attention, Raintree." The captain's eyes narrowed.

"Sorry."

Kingsman's right. I'm not fully awake. Not to mention the hand job I gave myself hadn't satisfied me. I sit straighter. "Go on."

Kingsman smirked. "The FBI has a missing person and wants our help."

I shrugged. "People go missing all the time."

"Not one of their own," he counters. "A few weeks ago, the agent left a note on her SAC's desk informing him she had an emergency and needed an extended leave. No one's heard from her since. They're not sure she's still alive."

"Why is a missing FBI agent the Bureau of Organized Crime's problem?"

"Since her prints were found at a BOC crime scene—one of Vasily Savin's cells."

Savin ran a sex-traffic auction for the Russian Mob. Now he's buried six feet under.

"We rescued those women." I was being a total ass, but that's what happened after spending the night on my couch and having dreams of Jess interrupted. Hell, who was I kidding? I'm always an ass. I haven't slept in the bed Jess and I shared since I left her behind thinking it was the only way to protect her. Two fuckin' years later and I'm still sleeping in the guest room or crashing on the couch.

"I understand you're still pissed that the Bureau didn't follow through with your suggestion that an inside leak sabotaged your last mission with them. Let it go, Raintree."

Easy for him to say.

Kingsman steepled his fingers. "According to Special Agent in Charge, Reynolds, the missing agent wasn't with the women we rescued during the raid. She's your old partner."

I had one partner while I was with the FBI. My gut churned and I lost the crappy attitude. "Fuck."

I'd like to cut him off, but I can't stop the next words that spilled from my captain's mouth. "Agent Jessica Lane."

"Son. Of. A. Bitch." It felt like a five-ton boulder was crushing my chest. I could barely breathe.

"I know you and Reynolds didn't part on good terms. I explained Abrams was out of pocket and you'd be taking the case. He wanted Abrams on this, but as you know, he's rented a condo in Florida while Jillian mends." Kingsman gave me a second. "This is too serious to wait."

Savin shot Tuck's woman a few weeks ago. It fucked Tuck up big time, and he'd taken Jillian away to heal both physically and emotionally. "Understood. Don't call him in."

"It may be too late to help Reynold's agent. You worked with Abrams on the case. I want you to handle it."

After the way I'd left Jess, I doubt she'd welcome my help. She may still star in my dreams, but I'm sure I'm number one on her shit-list. Had Savin auctioned her off like a piece of meat? "I'm on it. I need details."

"We don't have much to go on. Once we had hard evidence we were dealing with a sex-trafficking ring and could make the charges stick, we sent the case files to the FBI to review."

"In other words, you informed them about the raid *after* arrests were made?"

"Exactly." Kingsman leaned back and crossed his arms.

"Bet the FBI took that well." I wasn't surprised he'd limited the op to the BOC Unit. Kingsman didn't like to share with the FBI.

"I don't give a rat's ass. They've been pissed at me since the day I stole their top agent."

Kingsman hadn't *stolen* me from the FBI. After almost getting Jess killed, I'd decided to leave. It was a fluke Kingsman's offer came around the same time. In the field, I was continually distracted when she was near. I had a need to protect her instead of doing my job. Jess and I couldn't work together as long as I remained in love with her. This meant I'd never work with her again. God knew, I'd love that woman until the day I die.

I couldn't work with her, but I could damn-well rescue her. "Details?"

Kingsman tapped the papers before him. "While reviewing the files, the FBI noticed a statement from a woman we interviewed after our raid of Savin's home. She'd said Agent Lane is a friend and had been imprisoned with her." Kingsman ran a finger down the papers. "She stated Lane had been removed from the cells, kicking and screaming the day before our team's raid."

My gut roiled knowing Jess had been locked inside Savin's cells. He was the lowest of all the human traffickers the BOC had dealt with. The thought of Jess in the hands of men who auctioned women as sex-slaves would've sent me to my knees if I hadn't been sitting. I find a small amount of hope knowing Jess is a fighter. She won't make things easy for the bastards.

Still, my girl's in trouble. My girl? I have no claim on her. "We missed her by one goddamned day?"

"Looks that way. The FBI forensics people hacked into the Russian's computer and pulled up the files with the name of the man who'd picked Lane up."

"Why didn't Savin keep her for the auction?"

"Apparently, she'd been a pain-in-the-ass. They sold her early."

She'd already been sold. Her fiery temper had made things worse. I closed my eyes, trying to fight back an angry scream. "What's the fucker's name?"

"Cory Morris, a real douchebag, mob-wanna-be, from the North Side. We don't have the name of the actual buyer." Kingsman shoved the papers inside the file folder.

"Having a name is a start." I'll track the bastard down and make him talk.

"Exactly."

"Is the FBI letting me handle this without interference?" No matter what had gone wrong in our past, I won't trust anyone else to save Jess.

"Reynolds is giving you forty-eight hours. In return, he wants updates when available."

"Isn't that generous?" Reynolds knew I wouldn't welcome his help. Not after the last op Jess and I worked had been compromised by someone in the fucking FBI. I lost three teammates and Jess almost died. In the end, I'd lost her anyway. Reynolds had a mole, but never followed up on my hunch. Maybe Reynolds was the leak?

Kingsman tossed me the folder. "Morris was only the man sent to fetch her. It's been a couple weeks, but if the buyer lives in the US, you have a chance of extracting her."

"Assuming she doesn't get herself killed fighting back." A thought came to me. "Captain, if Jess was taken before the raid, she'd doesn't know her friend's been rescued, or that we know she was sold. She'll think she's on her own and will fight every inch of the way."

"I agree." Kingsman stood. "Sorry, there's no additional information on Lane's whereabouts."

"Thanks, Captain. Maybe, if her buyer lives here and she's behaving, I'll find her in one piece."

I knew deep in my soul, that was one fuckin' big *maybe*.

Chapter Two

Jessica

My body hurt, especially my shackled wrist. I'd tugged on the chain until my wrist was a bloody mess. I'd never show the bastard holding me how much pain I was in. I may have made a minor tactical error by going out on my own to rescue Lindy from the sex-trafficking Russians. Okay…make that a *major* tactical error. Yes, yours truly, Agent Jessica Lane, made a mistake.

As it turned out, being a pain-in-the-ass while being held captive in the Russian's cells hadn't been a great plan either. I thought back to just how big of a PITA I'd been…

After dragging information from one of my CI's, I'd hung around the bar where Lindy was last seen; hoping whoever had taken her would notice me. After four nights of sitting in a known hangout of the Russian Mafia, wearing a tight, up-to-my-ass-cheeks dress, a man dressed in a thousand-dollar suit made a move.

"Can I buy you a drink?" He'd asked, his Russian accent strong.

"Sure," I answered. He took the seat next to me and scooted close.

Then he bought me a second drink and slipped a roofie into my third. I'll admit, when the drug began to take effect, I had a few moments of pure panic. By then it was too late. My rescue plan had been already put in motion.

I came to again as a man tossed me into a cage with other women. Obviously some had been in the cells a while. Their blank eyes spoke to me. They'd given up on being rescued. A few others still showed signs of hope.

My heart raced when I spotted Lindy. Her eyes were dull with defeat until she saw me.

Lindy crawled on all fours to me and wrapped me in a tight embrace, tears streaming down her face. "Thank God, Jessie. When are your FBI friends coming to save us? I can't take much more of this craziness. These bastards plan to auction us." Her voice was raw.

"Shhh. No one can know I'm FBI. They'll kill me in a heartbeat if they do."

"Sorry. You're right." Lindy wiped her tears away with her palms. "So, when are they coming?"

How in the hell was I supposed to answer? Because of my bad decision to go out on my own, no one was coming to help any of us. I'd have to do this on my own. All I needed was a good plan, a big gun, and possibly the keys to our cells. Easy-peasy.

"I'm afraid we're on our own," I admitted.

Lindy's shoulders sagged.

The door to the cell squeaked open and a guard stepped inside. Without a second thought I charged, head-butting him in his gut. Before I could grab his weapon, a second man came in and put me in a headlock.

The room spun. I was going to die.

Everything went black.

"Wake up, Jessie," Lindy whispered. "You're okay."

"I'm not dead?"

"No. Anton didn't want you dead, but he's pissed."

"Anton?"

"The boss of our guards." Lindy helped me sit up.

"Bratva Captain." I rubbed my throat. Maybe pissing the guards off would work. Or get me killed.

The next day, I threw my tray of food at a guard and spit on him. From then on, I continued to cause trouble. I had no idea how many days I'd been caged, but I wouldn't stop until I could no longer move.

***

"Please stop, Jessie. You're going to push the bastards too far," Lindy begged.

"I've got to attack them until I can catch one off-guard." Most of the Russian bastards sported a nice, deep scratch—or two, across their faces...courtesy of yours truly. "Why haven't they beaten, tasered, or shot me?" Anton only used a chokehold to render me unconscious.

"I'm not sure," Lindy said. "This isn't the way sex-traffickers normally treat their captives. A guard killed one of the women the same day Anton came. Since then, we've been fed twice a day, offered water regularly, and given fresh-wipes."

"Anton must set the rules." He didn't allow the guards to sexually molest us much less rape us. Their slow smiles and the way they tended to undress us with their eyes made my skin crawl. They wanted to sample the goods. Apparently, they'd feared the wrath of Anton more. Clearly, Anton didn't trust his men. He'd slept on a cot in an area where a table and chair were. Did he want to keep a close eye on us—or perhaps on his men?

Anton didn't come across as evil as the rest of the Bratva. Sometimes he had kind eyes but immediately turned on the bad-ass glare if his men were present. He was huge and I had to admit, handsome, in a rugged sort of way. I doubt he had to buy women at an auction.

Still, he was a kidnapper and didn't release the women no matter how much they begged. He was no better than the rest. If I get the chance, I will punch the shit out of that handsome face of his.

"I've pushed the other dickheads to the max with my attacks." My energy and ideas were close to being depleted. "I only needed one guard to lose control. I'll knock him on his ass, slip past him, and play the rest by ear."

"You're going to get yourself killed," Lindy pointed out for the hundredth time.

***

Several days later, Anton, who rarely left the cell area except for a quick shower, was needed upstairs. He left one of his men in charge. Excitement snaked up my spine. This could be my chance.

"Lindy, I think I can get us out if you'll help me." I kept my voice low.

"Anything you need, Jessie."

"Good. I'm going to kill you."

Lindy's eyes widened. "You're what?" She stepped backward.

"It'll be an act. I'll pretend to choke you, and you'll fake like you're dying."

Lindy moved forward again. "And then?"

"Hopefully the guard will come into the cell to stop me, and I'll take him down." I'd tried to sound confident. In truth, I'd been locked up long enough to have lost weight and had no clue if I could pull it off. I had to try something, though.

"Are you sure? They have guns, and they're big men."

"I kick ass when it comes to hand to hand combat. Plus, Anton threatened the guards with death if they damage the merchandise. We're worth big money."

"We should do it now before Anton, or another guard, comes back," Lindy said enthusiastically.

"Love you, girlfriend," I whispered before I grabbed her by the neck and yelled, "I told you not to get in my face. You're gonna die, bitch."

"Fuck you," Lindy yelled back. I'd never heard her drop an F-bomb. If the situation hadn't been so grave, I likely never would've.

"I don't do women." I put her in a headlock and pretended to choke her. A few of the other women in our cell gathered around.

The guard ran to the cell, yelling at me in Russian. He'd waved his gun around but didn't fire.

Lindy slapped at my hands and made a good show of it. She'd kicked her legs and flopped around like a fish out of water. She was good at being murdered. If we somehow manage to survive, I'll encourage her to consider an acting career.

With a few well-placed grunts, she went limp, faking her demise.

I turned to lay her down, my back to the guard. I braced myself for him to enter the cell and come close enough I could take him down. I needed him to make his move before other guards arrived...or worse, Anton showed up.

Finally, his keys jingled. I clenched my hands into tight fists, ready to strike. Before I had a chance to turn around, a gazillion knives stabbed at the center of my back. The bastard tasered me? My extremities twitched, and Lindy slipped to the floor. I'd hit the ground next to her and convulsed.

In my peripheral vision, I'd watched in horror as a second guard came at me with a syringe. The needle stung like a bitch. Then Anton appeared and punched the guard holding the syringe in the face.

Well that didn't go quite the way I'd planned, I thought, as everything faded to black.

***

Now, here I am, chained to a bed, inside an almost dark room. It's so quiet I know the other women, including Lindy, aren't here. Once more, I have no idea if I've been out of it for a few weeks, a few days, a few hours, or mere minutes.

All I know is I'm in some serious shit.

Chapter Three

Tommy

I yanked Gregor's head back and put him in a choke hold. "Tell me where I can find Morris and I might let you breathe to pollute the air another day."

"I can't, Raintree. Morris will kill me if I do." Gregor reeked of alcohol and stale cigarettes. He'd been hiding since the raid at Vasily Savin's mansion. "Please—"

"Fuck Morris. Time to start thinking about the here and now. If you don't start talking in one minute, I'm gonna kill you. Maybe you should worry about me first."

"He'll kill me. You...won't 'cause you're a cop," Gregor huffed.

"Wrong, Gregor. I'm not a cop today. This is personal." Wanting him to see just how serious I am, I yanked his head upward. My don't-piss-me-off-again look was fuckin' scary and would get results.

"Okay. Okay. Morris never left Chicago. His boss was delayed by overseas business and is running a couple weeks behind."

"That's a fuckin' big delay. Keep talking." I gave his neck a little more pressure.

"He's hiding in an old warehouse two blocks from Lake Michigan. As of last week, he still had the woman. She's alive."

Chicago had dozens of warehouses near the Lake. "Which warehouse?"

"I'm not sure. A Russian company bought it twenty-something years ago to store electronics and other stolen shit they were shipping out of Chicago." Gregor's sweaty neck was getting harder to hang on to. "I promise that's all I have."

I pulled a zip-tie from my pocket and slapped it on him. I dragged him to a street sign, and used a second zip-tie, to secure him to the metal pole. I grabbed my phone and hit Kingsman's number.

"Captain, I've got one of Savin's guys tied to a sign pole ready for pickup." A few of the bastards who'd escaped the raid were still running loose in the city. I'm glad I was able to track Gregor down and pull the info I needed.

"I'll have some uniforms pick him up," Kingsman said.

"I need a list of all the warehouses sold to Russian companies from twenty-odd years ago and located within a few blocks of Lake Michigan."

"Is it still owned by them?"

"Possibly. I don't know if the place is occupied or deserted. Look, Captain, I know my information is vague, but our computer guys rock. They'll come through."

"I'll let you know what they find."

"Thanks."

"Give me the address for the pick-up."

I gave Kingsman the cross streets where he could find Gregor and disconnected, happy to know this piece of shit would soon join some of his Russian Mafia friends behind bars.

I kicked the sole of Gregor's shoe. "Your ride will be here soon. Sit back, take in the scenery, and relax. Think about the long, endless days you'll spend locked-up behind bars."

"Wait." He tugged on the hand restraints. "You promised you'd let me go if I told you what you wanted."

"Wrong. I promised I'd let you *live*. Didn't say anything about letting you go." I wiped my forearm, still damp from holding his wet and slimy neck, on my jeans.

"They'll kill me if you lock me up." Fear filled his voice.

"Dude, you stink. Ain't nobody gonna come near you, much less touch you. You oughta give up the smokes and vodka. Maybe take a shower...or twenty."

"You may as well shoot me now." The man was crying—actually crying.

The tough mafia guy was a pussy.

"Not gonna happen. But I promise to come back and kill you if you've given me bullshit information." If he's lying about the buyer being delayed, Jess might already be gone.

When Gregor didn't flinch at my threat, I was sure he'd given me everything he knew.

I moved toward my car at a quick pace. I'd parked a few blocks away hoping that Gregor wouldn't see me coming and rabbit. I'd cornered him near the viaduct he'd been camping beneath. As I walked, my mind turned to the story Tuck told me about a dead woman he'd seen dragged from Savin's cells the day he'd been made Bratva Captain, in charge of the cells.

The woman wasn't Jess. Thank fuck she hadn't landed herself inside Savin's cells until a week afterward. It didn't mean Morris wouldn't kill her. A shudder racked my body at the thought of my Jess being dead. I kicked up my pace. The sooner I find her the better.

I got in my car and drove like my ass was on fire to the warehouse district Gregor described. I hoped the BOC computer geeks could narrow my search to places matching Gregor's shitty description of possible locations. If not, I'd tear through every warehouse in the area. If I had to, I'd search all the fucking warehouses in Chicago.

I'll find Jess...or die trying. My life won't be worth Jack-shit if I couldn't tell her how much I need her back in my world. I fucked up and wanted a do-over. I'd even checked up on her from time to time. She'd been on a few dates, but nothing serious had ever developed with another man. Except for a fellow FBI agent, she'd only gone on one date with each man. I hoped it meant she was somehow still in love with me.

My phone vibrated in my jean's pocket. I pulled it out and checked the caller ID. "What've you got for me, Captain?"

"We have four possible locations. I'll text the addresses to you and call in SWAT. Don't approach the warehouses until back-up arrives."

"Copy that." I had no intention of doing so. Every second Jess spends with Morris, or worse her buyer, was one second too much.

"I mean it, Raintree. Wait for SWAT. We have no idea if Morris is alone or has other men with him.

Start with the first address on the list. The SWAT team will meet you there."

I disconnected. Two minutes later, the captain's texts came through with the addresses. It'd take SWAT ten minutes to load up and head out. In Chicago traffic, it'd take another fifteen to twenty to reach the warehouse area.

No fuckin' way would I wait.

Chapter Four

Jessica

A streak of glaring light fell across the floor before hitting my face. The sudden brightness hurt my eyes. My bloody wrist burned like a son-of-a-bitch from the handcuffs around it. In the muted light I could see the silhouette of a man shuffling toward me. Looked like he has a big-ass gun dangling from one hand and something resembling a rag in the other. I forced myself off the bed.

I'd fallen asleep—no I'd been drugged. I'd dreamed I was home, and in my bed, with the man I would love forever, even if he didn't return my feelings. In the dream, I was making love with Tommy when I should've been concentrating on an escape plan.

Sadly, my dream was just that. A dream.

"Take off your clothes, bitch. Your owner is coming tonight. I gotta hose-off the filth from your body." He tossed a towel and tiny sequined cocktail dress on the bed. "Put this on."

I held up the small scrap of red sparkly material and tossed it back to him. He batted it away.

"Sorry, dick-face. Turn around and crawl back into the hole you climbed out from. I'm not in the mood to go dancing. I sure as hell won't wear that crap."

"You need to follow orders. Put it on."

"That's a hard no." I yanked on the chain tethering me to the rickety bed. It's bolted to the floor. "Besides, I can't take off, or put on, anything while wearing this lovely piece of jewelry." I held up my hand.

He pulled something from his pocket and moved within a few inches of my reach. Dammit, not a key, but another syringe. Probably more knock-out drugs. "I'm going to become an addict at this rate."

I crouched, ready to fight. He deflected my swing and whacked me on the left side of my head with his gun. I bounced against the side of the bed and fell onto the floor. I barely had time to flip him off before he shot me with a drug. He started kicking me in the belly. I wrapped my free arm around my middle. Damn that shit hurt.

"Your boss isn't gonna like finding his merchandise damaged. You just fucked yourself." My words slur, and I'm fading fast.

At least I got to see a look of horror blanket his ugly face before I passed out.

***

Tommy

"Way to waste time, Raintree." Speaking to myself was never a good sign. The first warehouse I checked out was a bust. It was big with cobwebs and mouse shit all over the inside. There were no signs of any humans having stepped foot inside for at least ten— or twenty, centuries. I hadn't made it halfway through when my cell phone vibrated in my pocket. After checking caller ID, I ignored it. Kingsman was only calling to chew my ass out for not waiting for back-up.

Yeah, call me a rebel. Disobeying orders will likely get me busted back to a CPD uniform on foot patrol for the inconceivable future or working as a high school security officer. But if it meant getting Jess away from the man—or men—holding her even a minute sooner, I'd do it.

I parked by the next warehouse, pulled out my gun, and crept to the back entrance. After picking the lock, I entered quietly. Muffled chatter came from an office several feet to my right. Something along the lines of, the gig was supposed to be a few days, not weeks. It had to be Morris. Judging by the heated one-sided conversation, he was arguing on a phone—or with his schizophrenic asshole self.

I scooted along the wall, ready to fire on Morris if he came out of the room. I was almost to the door when he lets out a loud 'fuck you', followed by a clattering noise, and the stomping and crackling of plastic breaking. The man just killed his phone.

He was pissed.

He stepped out of the office and froze when he saw my 9mm pointing his direction. Saying he's surprised to find me is an understatement. After a nanosecond of looking shocked, he started to reach inside his suitcoat pocket.

I aimed my gun at his face, shaking my head. "Don't."

He seemed to contemplate his chances of drawing his weapon and firing before I blow him away. His eyes narrowed, and he raised his hands.

"Good choice, Morris."

"Why are you holding a gun on me? I've done nothing wrong." He looked behind him nervously. "And how the fuck do you know me?"

"I have your mug shot on my phone." I take a step closer. "Is she in there?"

"Who?" Morris responded, his voice shaky.

"Jessica Lane. You know who I'm talking about." I smiled at him. "In case you're not sure, she's a feisty redheaded *FBI agent*."

The color drained from his face.

"Didn't know you and your boss bought a federal agent? Oh man. Sucks to be you." I wagged my gun at him.

"I...I...I didn't know she's FBI."

"Would it have mattered?" Morris didn't answer. "Yeah, I didn't think so."

"She's okay. I swear. She has a few bruises here and there, but nothing a little make up won't cover."

I roared and charged. We both went down onto the cold concrete floor. I landed on top and slammed a fist into his gut, knocking the air from his lungs. I raised my gun to go a few rounds with his face and realized he was finished for now. As much as I'd love to kill him, I needed him alive. I wanted details on his boss.

I removed Morris's gun from a holster and tossed it. After securing his hands and feet with zip-ties, I hopped up and ran into the room, terrified of what I might find. It's mostly dark, but I could make out a figure on the bed. Using the flashlight on my phone to find a light switch, I flipped it on.

Jess is on a bed, wearing some sort of red sequined thing. I think it's a dress. It's pretty fuckin' small. A pair of matching heels are on the floor nearby. One hand is chained to the headboard, and she's not moving. I swallowed hard a few times.

"Dammit!" I ran to Morris and searched his pockets for the key to the handcuffs.

"She better fucking be alive," I said to the limp pile of shit on the floor, emphasizing my words with a kick to his gut.

Settling on the right side of the bed, I see she's breathing. My heart raced as I gently released her hand from the cuffs. Her wrist was bloody and bruised. My Jess fought hard to break free. I kissed the inside of her wrist. "I'm so sorry, darlin'."

She moaned and her head rolled towards me. Pushing her hair away from her face, I ground my teeth and bit back a wave of panic and anger. The whole left side of her face was one massive bruise. Her eye was swollen shut. Fucking Morris. I needed to finish beating the shit out of him. Or perhaps planting a bullet between his eyes would be more satisfying.

Chapter Five

Jessica

My stomach hurt, and the left side of my face was on fire. Holy shit, what had happened? Needing to see where I was, I tried to open my eyes. My left eyelid was stuck together. My right eye was okay, but I found myself staring into the deep blue orbs of a face I'd loved for six years. I hadn't seen him in almost two, but I'd never forget his eyes.

"Tommy?" I managed to croak past my dry, cracked lips. Damn my body ached.

"Yeah, darlin', it's me." His eyes watered.

"Is it really you?"

"In the flesh." His lips skimmed over the inside of my wrist, and he brushed another light kiss on my forehead. "Tell me what hurts."

Only everything. It took a minute to pull myself together before I spoke. "Besides the obvious, I'd say my heart."

Panic blanketed Tommy's face. "Like a heart attack?"

"No. Like a broken heart." I shouldn't do this now, but I couldn't seem to shut my mouth. I'd wanted answers for so long. I didn't care if the timing was off. For all I knew, Tommy would take off again now that I was awake.

"I'm—"

"Let me finish, Tommy." Words poured from me unchecked. "Where were you after I was shot two years ago? Didn't you think I deserved better than Reynolds giving me your verbal *Dear John* letter?" I rubbed the old scar on my belly.

"I know I handled things the wrong way." He shook his head. "I'm sorry, but I almost got you killed. My head wasn't in the game the day you were shot. You almost paid the ultimate price for my fuck-up. "

"What're you talking about? A low-life trafficker shot me."

"I should've noticed the shooter wasn't dead."

"He had a Kevlar vest under his shirt."

"I didn't see him move. You did."

"You didn't see it, Tommy, because I drew your attention away when I waved at you. You weren't facing the right direction to see him because of me. It was *my* fault, if anyone's. Not yours."

"I should've been aware of all my surroundings. The only thing I was aware of at that moment was my fucking dick and making jokes."

"Why didn't you stay and talk things through?" A tear rolled down my cheek, and I wiped it away.

"I didn't deserve you if I couldn't keep you safe."

"Bullshit." Now he was starting to piss me off. "I don't want to talk about this anymore. Get me out of here."

Tommy helped me stand, and I glanced down at an itchy, sequined red dress the size of a hankie I'm wearing. My hair was damp. Morris had knocked me out and hosed me down after all. A shiver raced through me. I bent over and threw up a ton of nasty-tasting bile. I couldn't remember the last time I'd eaten or had a drink. My vomit landed on top of a pair of hooker fuck-me-heels, and I started to dry-heave.

I wasn't sure if the nausea was from the stomach pain, the thought of Morris seeing me naked and touching me, or the reality that I'd come fucking close to becoming some sick bastard's sex-slave.

I straightened and realized Tommy was standing close, holding my hair back while I humiliated myself. He pulled a handkerchief from his pocket and handed it to me.

"It's going to be okay. Let's go." Tommy's voice was low and shaky. I'd heard that tone before when he was angry and about to lose his shit. I knew his rage wasn't directed at me.

"I'm okay." I said the words like I believed them. It's all bullshit. Turning to face him, I saw the same fury I'd heard a moment before. Then sadness filled his eyes. After all this time, seeing me in pain still hurt him.

I lost it, bursting into tears. When Tommy pulled me into his arms, I went without hesitation. I should've kept my distance to protect my heart and sanity.

But since when did I ever do what was best for me?

Chapter Six

Tommy

I soaked up the warmth of Jess in my arms again. It's like coming home. She belonged to me, and I'd been a fucking fool to try and distance myself from her. She was right. I should've stayed and worked things out.

I could've gone to work at the Chicago PDBOC while she stayed with the FBI. There must've been a thousand better ways to handle it. But I'd been too upset with myself to be reasonable.

I stepped away from her embrace and took her hand. She didn't yank it away from my hold or kick me in the balls. Surely that's a good sign. The sooner we got out of there, the quicker I could beg her to give me another chance.

We walked through the door, still holding hands. She stiffened for a moment then moved next to the zip-tied Morris. He'd regained consciousness and curled into himself. I'd be scared too if Jess was standing over me, shooting daggers.

"You drugged me, took off my clothes, and hosed me down like a damned animal." She reared back a bare foot and kicked the bastard in his nuts.

"Ouch," I said. "You pissed off the wrong woman."

"Fuck you," Morris screamed and covered his balls with his restrained hands.

Before Jess could kick him again, a door squeaked open. We turned at the same time. Jess's jaw dropped, and she stumbled backward against me. "What the hell," she mumbled. "Glen, it's Jessica Lane. Put the gun down."

FBI Agent Glen Collins stood before us, pointing a gun in our direction. Obviously, he wasn't here to help.

"Surprised to see me?" Collins asked.

"What're you doing here, Collins?" I tightened my hold on my Sig.

"Came to pick up my merchandise." He waved his gun at Jess. "Step over here, Jessica. I own you now."

"You're the bastard who bought me?"

"In the flesh. Now move it, or I'll kill Raintree. I never understood what you saw in him."

Jess ignored his request, and I pulled her behind me. "Fuck you, Collins. There's no way you're walking away with Jess."

"And I'm not about to let you die for me," Jess murmured into my back, and her warm breath washed over my skin.

Shit, here we go again.

"We'll do this together. When I say jump, we leap to opposite sides. I'll go left and take the shot." My voice was barely a whisper. Hopefully, she heard me.

"But—" Her voice was louder. Yep, she heard.

"Non-negotiable, Jess." I kept mine low. Neither one of us needed to die. "My aim is rock-solid."

"Quit whispering and toss the gun, Raintree." Collins took a step closer.

We needed to keep him talking until SWAT arrives. "When did you go bad, Collins?" I asked.

"Years ago. You'd be surprised what people will pay for information."

"Are you the one who leaked the info on our trafficking raid two years ago?" Jess asked.

"Right under Reynold's and everyone else's nose."

"You got most of our team killed. I almost died." Bitterness filled Jess's voice.

"You weren't supposed to be hurt. My guys were supposed to kill everyone *except* you. I wanted you even back then. I tried to get you to date me after Raintree left. That didn't work either."

Jess shook her head.

"Then I saw you up for sale on a Russian's sex-slave site a few weeks ago and boom, you're finally mine."

"What the fuck were you doing on their auction site?" My hands twitched, the need to strangle Collins strong.

"I purchase a new sex-slave every few months. Normal women are weak and don't last very long. A trained FBI agent like Jessica should give me months of pleasure." Collins took another step. "Let's go, Jessica. There's a boat waiting for us. Be good, and I'll kill Raintree with a head-shot. He doesn't need to suffer."

"Cut my zip-ties, Collins," Morris said. Hell, I'd forgotten about him.

"I'm no longer in need of your services." Collins aimed his gun at Morris and fired. When Morris was silenced for good, he turned back to them. "I can tell by Jessica's face that Morris manhandled my merchandise. She didn't come cheap."

Collins killing Morris was an opportunity I didn't see coming. "Jump!" I yelled to Jess.

We dove to the floor. I fired my Sig three times on the way down, and Collins dropped.

I jumped up and checked on Collins. Jess moved to my side. "Can't get any deader than that, darlin'," I said.

"I can't believe this is the son-of-a-bitch who killed our team."

"Fuck, Jess. He almost got you killed that same day." A shiver curled up my spine at the thought.

I checked Morris's pulse. Nothing.

Jess kicked Collin's body. "Yeah, he's dead." I guess she needed to double-check.

The door swung open again, and I aimed my gun.

Kingsman's SWAT team had arrived. I slowly laid down my weapon. Jess and I both held up our hands. "I'm BOC," I yelled and shifted my right hip in their direction showing them the CPDBOC badge clipped to my belt. "Thomas Raintree."

"FBI Agent Jessica Lane," Jess said. She had no credentials with her, but that shouldn't be a problem.

"You're both good," the SWAT guy who seemed in charge said. "I'm Donaldson."

Jess and I put down our hands.

I picked up my 9mm and tucked it into my holster. "That dead piece of shit back there is Cory Morris. The other hunk of dead shit, is dirty FBI Agent, Glen Collins."

"Kingsman filled us in on Morris. Your captain asked me to relay a message." I know exactly what Kingsman's message entailed.

"Yeah, I bet he did."

"He said to get your ass back to the station ASAP."

"Got it."

Donaldson pointed to Jess. "She gonna need EMT support?"

Jess was swaying, looking seconds away from hitting the floor. Her adrenalin rush was over, and she was crashing. I scooped her up in my arms and took off. "It'll be faster for me get her to the hospital. Thanks for the assist."

"I'll fill Kingsman in," Donaldson said.

I didn't bother to answer. There's one thing on my mind and that's getting Jess out of this fucking warehouse. Her eyes fluttered closed. I hugged her to my chest tighter, noting she weighed next to nothing.

***

Using my lights and siren, I made it to the hospital in record time. I was met by a couple nurses with a stretcher. They opened the passenger side door and I yell, "She's a federal agent."

"We've got her," one of them said. They loaded her onto the gurney, started taking vitals, and rushed her inside.

I pulled my car forward, leaving my flashing lights on. I ignored the woman sitting at the ED's front desk and ran straight to the cubicles. I could tell by the flurry of action where they had Jess. My heart skipped a beat when I saw the number of people working on her and how pale she was.

They started an IV and a doctor issued orders. Labs were drawn and a portable X-ray machine was brought in. I stepped out of the room and called Kingsman. He had a good time chewing my ass out after I updated him. I got lucky, and he didn't bust me back to a uniform.

Kim, a nurse I'd met through Tuck's girl and dated a few times, took me by the arm and led me from the room. "She's in good hands."

"I know she is, Kim. I can't help worrying."

"Is she the one?" Kim asked as she sat me down on a chair outside Jess's cubicle.

"Yeah. I'm going to do everything I can to win her back."

"When we dated, you were always upfront with me that your heart belonged to another woman." She said. "I'm glad you've decided to try and mend things with her. But hey, if it doesn't work out, you've got my number." She gave my hand a squeeze and went back inside Jess's room.

I sat on the chair praying Jess would be okay, and she'd take me back. An hour later, her doctor came out.

"Agent Lane should be okay. She's suffering from severe dehydration and a mild concussion. X-rays show no broken bones on her face where she's been hit. I've ordered a CT scan to check for brain injury and one for the spleen."

"Brain injury?" That shit didn't sound good. "Spleen?"

"The brain scan is a precaution since she arrived unconscious. She's awake now and talking, so I expect a negative CT scan. She's not showing indications of a ruptured spleen, but she's taken multiple kicks in the abdomen. Never hurts to double check."

"I want to see her again."

"She's going for the CT scan in a few minutes. You can sit with her until then."

"Jess doesn't go anywhere without me."

He nodded. "I'll let the staff know."

***

According to the CT scan, Jess didn't have a brain bleed or ruptured spleen. She's only said a few words to me. For the most part, they consisted of, "Isn't it time for you to run away and hide?" Or, "Don't you have somewhere else to be?" And other similar insults. I'd earned her attitude and accepted them. She was rightfully pissed about my disappearing act two years ago.

After eight hours of fluids, Jess's color had returned, and she'd eaten every small meal they'd offered. She was antsy to be released. Her boss and several of her co-workers came by, but only SAC Reynolds was allowed in.

Shocking the holy-hell out of me, Reynolds told me the FBI and CPDBOC were working together to try and find other women the Russians had sold. Chances of recovery were slim, but they have Gregor in custody, and he was a blabbering idiot.

The doctor finally agreed to release Jess, but only if somebody stayed with her and kept an eye on her overnight. She wasn't going to like it, but I planned on being that somebody.

Chapter Seven

Jessica

I wasn't sure why Tommy insisted on hanging around. He either sat next my bed, or in a chair outside my cubicle. He'd made a couple trips to the waiting room to update agents who had stopped by. Once it was clear I was okay, they left.

If Tommy wanted to be there…fine. I'd make his life miserable.

"Can I get you a drink, darlin?" Tommy picked up a glass of water.

I gave him the evil eye.

"Tell me if you do." He leaned forward with his head down, his elbows on his knees.

Yes, it's petty of me. I loved seeing the look of guilt on his face each time I reminded him how he ran from me two years ago. I was being a bitch, but he'd earned my animosity.

I'd been lying in bed all day with my thoughts. I knew I should've moved on without Tommy. I'd tried and couldn't. He truly believed he was protecting me by leaving. It's asinine, but I understood his reasoning. I could've gone after him and insisted we talk things through, but I was stubborn.

I see things differently now. I'd almost became a sex-slave. I had concluded life is too short to not be with the man I love. I was going to give our relationship another chance but planned to make him work for it.

"How're you feeling, Agent Lane?" My boss said, interrupting my thoughts as he stepped into my room.

"I'm good, sir."

"You had us worried." Reynolds crossed his arms. "When you're cleared to come back to work, we'll discuss your actions in detail."

"I understand." My SAC wasn't about to let my little adventure slide.

"Do what the doctors say and get better." He patted my shoulder.

Reynolds moved to Tommy and shook his hand. "Thanks for the assist, Raintree."

It was surreal. He gave Tommy's shoulder a fatherly squeeze. Reynolds hadn't bothered to hide his anger when Tommy abruptly left the FBI. I guess finding out who the Bureau's snitch was made everyone happy.

I'd learned about a year ago that Reynolds and Tommy had quite an argument over whether the FBI had a leak. Tommy was right. Now the leak was plugged and the agent behind our ambush, Collins, was dead.

As soon as Reynolds cleared the room, my doctor entered. "You ready to go home?"

"Yes. If any more fluids are pumped into me, I'll drown."

"I'll fill out your release papers." He gave me discharge instructions, including the one that specified Tommy would be spending the night to watch over me. Apparently, concussions were tricky little shits.

***

Tommy

After we got home, Jess continued to ignore me. I'm out of mindless words that didn't need a response. I'd choke if I tried to apologize one more time for my past behavior. She was eating this shit up.

I made canned soup for dinner. "Here you go. Eat up. Tomorrow I'll do some grocery shopping." Jess needed real food to put on the weight she'd lost.

I needed beer if I were to have any chance of surviving her silent treatment.

After dinner, I plopped on the couch with the remote control. Jess locked herself inside her room. I'll give her tonight. She wasn't in any shape yet for me to bring on my A-game. But I would win her back.

I had to.

"I'm going to bed." Jess appeared and tossed a pillow and blanket at me.

"Don't lock your door again or I'll break it down. The doctor released you with the condition I check on you several times tonight."

"Okay." She started to leave but hesitated. "Can we talk?"

"I've been trying to talk to you all day."

"I know. I've had a lot to think about. I didn't want to talk until I was sure how I felt." She sat on the couch close enough to take my hand in hers. "Honest-to-God, I've tried to hate you."

"I've noticed." I snorted.

"The truth is I'll always love you." She scooted closer, erasing the gap between us.

"Does this mean you forgive me?"

"This means I'll *try* to forgive you. I've realized life is too short not to be with the man I love."

"I love you so fuckin' much, Jess." I gathered her in my arms.

"Our relationship needs work. You have to promise to never leave me again without talking first."

"I promise. Should we seal it with a kiss?"

"No."

My heart sank.

"Let's seal it by making love."

***

Jessica

My mind was made up and there's no going back.

I'm not sure why I gave in to Tommy so soon. I only know I want him in my life and in my bed. Now. "It's been too long."

"Way too long. Are you sure you're up to this, darlin'?"

It's nice he asked, but yes, I'm up for it. Judging by the bulge in his pants, he's up to it, too. "I'm good." I kissed him.

Tommy quickly took my kiss to a whole new level. I melted and relaxed into his embrace. He gathered me in his arms as if I were fragile and carried me to my bedroom. The mere thought of making love to him made my panties wet.

He set me on the bed and removed the sweatpants and tank top I'd put on after my shower. He tried to lay me down, but I pushed him away.

"Your turn."

The desire in his eyes brought on a whole new wave of wetness. Was it possible to have an orgasm just thinking about having him inside me?

I wanted to strip him slowly, but that shit wasn't happening. I tore off his clothes like a sex-starved maniac. Who was I kidding? I was a sex-starved maniac.

In the blink of an eye, he had me spread out on the bed, kneeling between my legs.

I moaned.

"Oh, darlin'. I didn't think you could be anymore beautiful than before." He leaned over me and nibbled on my neck. "I was fuckin' wrong."

"I know how you feel." I didn't think Tommy's muscles could be bigger than two years ago, but his six-pack had morphed into an eight-pack.

"God, woman, I love you." He kissed his way down to my breasts and began swirling his tongue over one and then the other. My pebbled nipples grew impossibly harder as he blew on them and gently bit on the tight peeks.

"Tommy." My voice came out gravelly.

"I've dreamed of this so many times. You're perfect in every way possible," he said.

He slid his lips southward. His callused hands massaged my inner thighs in slow, sensual circles. He spread my legs, giving his mouth full access to my sweet spot. With one long stroke of his magic tongue, my orgasm burst loose.

"Tommy," I screamed.

He didn't give me a chance to come down before he rose above me and plunged inside me. "You feel so damned good, darlin'."

I'd forgotten how much I loved him calling me darlin'.

"I love you," he whispered against the sensitive curve between my shoulder and neck, careful not to touch the damaged left side of my face.

"Love…you…too." I could hardly speak when he was inside me.

His strokes were long and slow, blending us into one person. I was close to climaxing again.

As if he could read me, he murmured, "Darlin', let go with me. I'm about to burst." I sucked at following orders but obeyed.

He grunted and stiffened as I hit my peak and I hung on for dear life until his warm semen emptied inside me.

We stayed wrapped in each other's arms for what seemed like hours.

"Darlin'," Tommy said hoarsely. "I didn't suit up. I lose control when I'm around you."

"I do the Depo shots. Standard FBI rules if you're in the field."

"I forgot." He ran a hand up and down my back.

"This is what I missed the most."

"The sex?"

"Yes, and the snuggling afterwards. I love your touch, Tommy."

He planted a few soft kisses on the injured side of my face. I could finally open my swollen eye. I studied my man and cupped his chin. "I should've hunted you down after I was released from the hospital two years ago."

He hugged me tighter. "I shouldn't have run, but I couldn't shake the fear of causing you any more pain, or getting you killed."

"We'll get it right this time. I'm not letting you go again."

"Ditto, darlin'. We've got this."

As Time Goes By

by

Maggie Adams

Chapter One

Elizabeth stared into the fire. It was mid-November in Highland, Illinois and cold inside the old house. Or maybe her shivering was because this day never failed to send her back to that moment when her husband Robert's supervisor, Peter Mitchell, stood at the door with a message. After he sat down in the living room away from prying eyes, he began, *"Mrs. Matthews, I'm sorry to inform you your husband was killed in action..."*

Three days later, Robert came home and was laid to rest. Her life took on a surreal intensity then. A representative from Homeland Security came and asked to see Robert's things. She was told he'd fallen from a building and broken his neck. He couldn't give her any more information, and he knew nothing of the whereabouts of his best friend, Thomas "Tank" O'Leary.

She buried her husband waiting in vain for some sign of Tank. He'd know what to do, why Homeland Security, the FBI, and NCIS had grilled her on Robert's habits. He'd be able to help her figure out exactly what had happened to her husband.

Tank never showed–not a word, a flower, a message, a call. Nothing for two years. She'd given up hope of ever truly finding out what had happened to Robert or why she'd been interrogated those first few months after his passing. She'd come upon dead end after dead end within the government. Except for his commanding officer, Peter Mitchell, no one wanted to tell her anything. Thankfully, Mitchell had proven to be a good friend, helping her with her inquiries. All she was told was Robert had been following a lead.

Now, on the anniversary of Robert's death, she was taking out the last box of his things. She'd remembered that Robert had made a hidey-hole in the laundry chute, but hadn't been able to open it, the emotions too raw then. She pulled out some old photographs of him and Tank, the quick stab of pain from Tank's indifference to Robert's death made her catch her breath. Tossing it to the side, she rummaged through the rest–a concert ticket, a playbill, and a card from Valentine's Day. There were some faded photographs, a few books he enjoyed as a child. She picked up the small bible, the old leather-bound book that he'd found in an antique shop. He'd always enjoyed illustrations. The bible was filled with such detailed work. Robert had told her it showed the devotion and love the artist wanted to convey.

She felt the tears fall from her blue eyes down her cheek and angrily brushed them away. With a deep breath to gather her strength, she said aloud, "I'll always love you, Rob, but I can't do this anymore. It's time to leave the past in the past and get on with my future."

She placed the items back inside a small box and picked up the bible once more. A slip of paper fell out. It was a picture of him and Tank in basic training. She flipped it over and found Robert's handwriting.

I want Tank to have this bible if anything happens to me. He would appreciate it.
-Robert.

Anger ripped through her. How dare he give Tank this bible! Tank deserved nothing. She shoved the picture and the bible back into the box and started to close the lid, but Robert's words haunted her. *If you're ever in trouble, call Tank, he'll know what to do.*

Well, Tank wasn't available. Tank didn't try to get in touch with her. *Tank didn't come to your funeral,* she screamed silently as tears ran down her cheeks. *Tank fuckin' left me alone just like you!* She shoved the box away, curling into a fetal position, her blonde hair falling around her, and sobbed. *God would this ever stop—the pain, the sorrow, the fear.*

After a few minutes, she dried her eyes. *The only way to get rid of the past was to bury it.* She grabbed the box and headed out the back door. Taking down a shovel, she dug between the beautiful rose bushes they had planted along the fence.

She took a moment to catch her breath and realized the hole was quite large. After tossing the box in, she began to fill it and then stomped on it, covering it with the mulch so it looked like it never existed. "There," She sighed, wiping the sweat from her brow. "No more past, only the future." With a renewed calm, she walked into the house and into the master bath, allowing the steaming water to cleanse her body and soul.

Chapter Two

Thomas "Tank" O'Leary set both feet firmly on the tarmac of Lambert International Airport. Finally, he was back where he belonged. All of the research, all of the clues, not to mention the months of hospitalization and the loss of his leg, had landed him here. He didn't know what he was going to do about Lizzie, but he did know one thing for certain, no way could she be a part of this mess, which meant she was in danger. He didn't know how much he should tell Lizzie and would have to choose his words carefully. There are still so many holes in Robert's death.

He pulled down her quiet street, parking across from Lizzie's home. The pale, yellow cottage still looked the same. Giant pots of geraniums and comfy chairs welcomed visitors on the porch. He noticed movement to the side of the yard. She was quietly tending her garden, instructing the little charges at her daycare on how to water and feed. Tank got out of the car thinking this might be the best way to approach her.

"Stranger danger! Stranger danger!" the little boy in the black and white striped shirt yelled as he ran around to Lizzie.

"Thank you, Joshua." She patted him on the back.

Tank watched her behind the veil of his sunglasses. She'd lost some weight, but she was still curvaceously beautiful. He felt his cock twitch. He'd always been attracted to her, but Robert had made the first move.

She approached the gate, her children behind her. "May I help you?" she inquired, the locked gate assuring her safety.

"Hello, Lizzie." He watched as recognition hit her blue eyes, the shock of seeing him making her gasp. Then her gaze scanned him from top to tail, traveling back up again. Their eyes met, fury igniting in hers. "Let me explain, Lizzie."

"Go away," she said firmly. She ushered the children back. "Kids, back inside."

"I'm sorry. I need to talk to you."

"Well, it's a little late to be offering condolences. I'm perfectly fine now. Thank you for stopping by." She followed the children.

He opened the gate and marched as quickly as his bum leg would carry him to her side, grasping her by the elbow. "You have to listen to me."

"No, I don't, Thomas. Whatever you had to say should've been said two years ago. I've managed to pick myself up and carry on." She wrestled away from him and ran inside, firmly closing the storm door.

He yelled, "I was in a foreign prison when Robert died. I lost my leg there." Tank wasn't leaving until she heard him out.

Elizabeth opened the storm door once again. "Come in but stay in the kitchen. I'll get you some tea. Let me settle the children for a nap. You can explain then."

He watched as she got out the tea and poured him a big glass with lots of ice, the children hovering at the kitchen door. "Go on now," she said to them. "You have five minutes to find your babies and your blankets. Rest time." The children hurried to find their things.

She set the tea down with the sugar bowl and a spoon. "Would you like something to eat? I could make you a sandwich." His stomach growled, and a smile tugged at her lips. "I'll take that as a yes." She quickly made him a sandwich and handed it to him with a bag of chips. He nodded gratefully, and she said, 'I'll be back."

He heard her instructing the children to lie down and soon, soothing music played over speakers. Little murmurs could be heard amidst the music, and the occasional shushing sound of Lizzie's soft voice urging the children into sleep.

While she was gone, he peered around the kitchen. She'd made some upgrades since the last time he was here, and it appeared she had completed all the tasks Robert had said they were working on.

Robert, what the hell happened? They had been so close to uncovering who was behind the heroin and trafficking distribution into the U. S., catching the guy from the Istanbul side. Robert had gone to meet the U.S. asset.

Robert, I don't think this is a good idea.

Look Tank, it's the only chance we've got. Everybody else is dead.

You asking to meet here in their territory was a bad idea. I've got a bad feeling. I don't think you should go.

I gotta go, we're meeting at 1500. I know you got my back. When this is all said and done, me, you and Lizzie will go on vacation. Maybe Aruba or somewhere else tropical.

You think Lizzie is gonna lay around on some beach? She'll have us hiking our asses off to some Scottish castle or running around England searching for some dead poet's tomb or something.

It's time.

"Thomas, wake up."

His eyes popped open, and he immediately became alert, staring into Lizzie's eyes.

"You fell asleep. Would you like to lie down in the guest room?"

"No. Are the kids down?" He passed a weary hand over his eyes.

"Yes, for the time being, so if you need to tell me something, you need to do it now," she replied bitterly. She sat across from him.

Gone were the warm smiles and the bright eyes he remembered from long ago. This woman had been through hell, her heart broken. You could see it in her face. She still had those crinkles of laugh lines near her eyes, but he didn't think she laughed much anymore. It was if she'd withdrawn into a protective shell. She looked fragile. "Lizzie, I didn't know about Thomas until six months ago. Since then, I've done everything possible to find out who was responsible. I don't know all of the facts, but I'm getting close. The clues led me here."

Lizzie nodded. She figured he was here for a reason, not because of her. "Where were you when he died?"

Like a burning ember shoved into his heart, her words pained him. Lizzie was always one to get right to the point. "I was doing my job. I thought I had everything under control. I had the proper vantage point where I could see Thomas and the meeting. They were at a local restaurant. Then I don't know what happened. I woke up in some prison overseas. My head was bashed in and my leg, well, let's just say it had seen better days. I was in and out of it for days. I heard one of my guards say they were killing the American tonight. Figured that meant me. I managed to escape, made it to the American Embassy, crawling to the gate and giving them my service number. The next thing I knew, I woke up in Walter Reed and doctors informed me I was assumed dead.

'That was six months ago. They took my leg, and I started prosthetic therapy as soon as I could, but I realized I wouldn't have much time. Someone in the agency wanted me dead. When my roommate in the hospital suddenly died of a heart attack, my inner voice told me to get the hell out. I got in touch with a friend in the Air Force I could trust, and he put me on a cargo plane, slipped me in with the luggage. I made my way here." He took a deep breath and blurted, "You're in danger."

"That's a lot to take in. I'm not sure what I can do or what this is about, but I'll do what I can." She set aside his theory about her being in danger. It had been two years. If someone was going to kill her, they'd had ample opportunity.

"What do you need? Is it money?" She jumped up from the table to put some distance between them. He'd not come back for her. She was simply another piece in the puzzle. He didn't even look like the old Tank. His dark hair was pulled back, his beard streaked with gray, but those amber eyes still pierced her soul. He was leaner, meaner...sexier. "I have a couple hundreds stashed. I can get more."

She rushed to the cookie jar. Tank rolled his eyes. The obvious place to put spare cash. "Why didn't you just put it in the freezer in a box of waffles?" he asked sarcastically.

Her eyes widened. "Because I read that's the first place a burglar looks."

He smiled at her answer and limped over to her, taking the cash and putting it back in the jar. "I need to find out if Thomas sent you anything or said anything to you?" *God, she is so pretty and sweet-smelling. I want to drag her upstairs and...*

He stepped back before he acted on his impulse. "Very few people knew where Thomas and I were going, and those are the people I'm looking into."

"You mean his supervisor? Peter's been great. He's been here for me. He helped me after and..."

Lizzie stopped, glancing up with scared eyes. "He helped me pack Robert's things. He said he'd haul them away." She slumped against the counter, turning white. "God, what have I done? No wonder they didn't need to kill me. I handed him everything with a goddamn bow on it!"

Tank took her hand. She was so trusting, so soft. "It's okay. I wasn't here to help you. I'm sorry about that." With a small tug, she was in his arms, her head against his chest. It felt so right. She was all that was good and honest in his world. "Even if Mitchell got one of Robert's ciphers, he couldn't decode it without the key."

She pulled back, a smile on her lips. "A cipher? Then maybe he didn't get everything." She spun out of his arms and headed out of the kitchen before he could ask what she meant. "I have to check on the children."

Thomas laid his hands on his head. He'd bungled this so badly. All the words he'd wanted to say, how she didn't need to be afraid, and now, she was probably terrified. Taking a deep breath, he set out to remedy this situation. His throat was suddenly parched, and his eyes darted to his empty glass. Shaking his head, he decided he wasn't going to encroach on her anymore. However, he didn't want to leave her like this, didn't want to leave this house. He just wanted it to be the way it was. *You're a fuckin' liar, Tank. You don't want it to be the way it was. You want it to be the way it could be now.*

He'd been in love with Elizabeth since he met her, but Robert had gotten to her first. At the time, he never thought he'd be good enough; hell, he still wasn't good enough for Elizabeth, yet here he was twenty years later, still in love. And there she was, standing in the doorway staring at him like he had two heads.

"I'm sorry, please sit." Tank turned back, motioning her to the bench.

Elizabeth took the seat she'd vacated a few minutes ago. "I believe you, Tank, but it's hard to fathom Peter as the enemy. Can any of this be checked?"

"No, all you got to go on is that I have been your friend for as long as you've known Robert."

"Robert said I could trust you." She took a deep breath. "I'm going to trust you, Tank, but if it turns out you had something to do with Robert's death, I will kill you."

She was such a tiny little thing, but the ferociousness of her tone said that she absolutely meant it. "I know, Lizzie. I thank God every day they didn't get to you."

"I wasn't even hiding. I guess they figured they had all of Robert's stuff and you were dead for all intents and purposes, so why bother with me?" She leaned in closer, and he did the same. "Except they didn't get all of it. Robert put a hidey-hole in the door of the laundry chute. I remembered it recently and checked it. I buried everything under the rose bush as a sort of closure."

He could hear the rustling in the other room. *Dammit!* The kids were up. He could tell she had more to say.

"Do you want some more tea?" she asked. "Help yourself and join me in the living room while I get the kids up. Grab those cookies, too, will you?"

"Sure." He grabbed the items, hoping the 'stranger danger' kid would cut him a break. He walked in, noting the changes. Gone was that big overstuffed leather recliner that Robert loved—it had his butt print in it. Now, there was a sleek sectional with a chaise on the end. A new television hung above the fireplace. She made it lovely, and he told her so.

"Thank you. It gave me something to do." She smiled a genuine smile for the first time since his arrival, which warmed his heart. "I redid every room and the yard. I also got a new car. Now I'm not sure what I'm supposed to do."

"As time goes by, it'll get better. At least, that's what they told me in the hospital." He awkwardly sat on the sofa. Conversations were never this hard with her.

"True. As time goes by, the pain lessens." She sat next to him, a brown-eyed baby in her arms. After a glancing briefly at him, the kids were more concerned with their cookies. "It's as if the memories take over. I'm sure there Robert will always be in my heart, but I've got to get on with my life."

"Absolutely, Lizzie. You're a beautiful woman with a kind heart. You have every reason to move on. Robert would want that."

She smiled softly. "Yeah, I know. Given his line of work, we had contingency plans. You know, I wasn't sure I'd stay, given all the memories here, and yet they are what kept me from leaving."

"I understand. This is where all the best memories I have are."

"I feel so many different emotions right now, Tank. I'm not sure what to do with them. I'm grateful that you are here and alive, and yet, I'm so angry that you are."

The pain of her words burned through him. "I'm alive, and Robert is dead."

"No, not at all." She shook her head. "I'd never wish such a thing, Tank. No, I'm angry that I spent two years angry with you because you just disappeared. My husband was dead. You were gone without a word. I got nowhere trying to get answers. Now I know why."

Tank grinned. "Well, they couldn't exactly say, 'Hey, Lizzie, we got him in a hospital, and we're going to kill him.'"

"Why didn't they kill you?" she asked.

"Too much red tape, I guess. It would look a little fishy if I suddenly died since the Embassy and the doctors were aware of my location."

Lizzie peered at the clock. "Well, if you don't want folks to realize you're in town, head upstairs. Parents will be coming soon."

124

"I'll be on my way then. I can grab a room at the bed and breakfast in town."

The myriad of emotions that crossed her face was almost comical. "Tibbetts House. Yeah, it's still here, but the lady who made all the nice chocolate retired to Boca Raton. So, all you're going to get is a lumpy mattress and a cold muffin," she said with a twinkle in her eye.

He grimaced, and she chortled, "Why don't you stay here?"

"If you're sure," he hedged.

"I'm sure." She stood up and hugged him. He could feel the warmth of her body through his cotton shirt. "Welcome home, Tank."

He felt tears well in his eyes.

"Thank you, Lizzie." He tried not to let the tears run, but he felt hers hitting his shirt.

She pulled back, and the moment was broken. "Look at us–a couple of weeping willows."

"I'm going to grab my stuff out of the rental car and head up." *God, that was lame, Tank.*

"Let's get an early dinner to celebrate my return. Okay?" He wrote on his hand and showed her. *Bugged?*

"Okay." She nodded. The knock on the front door was a welcome respite. Lizzie didn't want to examine why it felt so good to be in his arms.

Or why her body longed to press against him again.

"I'm bugged?" Lizzie asked taking a sip of the delicious Chardonnay. The Chop House was the swankiest place to eat in Highland. She thought Tank would appreciate a good steak.

"Yeah. Found one in the kitchen. And how long has that fancy school sign been there?"

Lizzie found the sudden change in subject odd. "It's been here about two years now."

He nodded as the entrée arrived. "Looks great," he said. "I walked over to it this evening. It's an optical bug. Mitchell and his goons have been watching you from a distance. But I've got a simple fix for that." He handed her the black and gold package.

"You brought me a present?"

"Well…"

She tore out the gold foil tissue paper and reached into the bag, pulling out a battery-operated purple vibrator. Her shocked expression of recognition and then her blush of embarrassment as she hastily stuffed it back into the bag had Tank chuckling.

She hissed at him. "What were you thinking? What is this for?"

"Well, normally it's—"

"I know what it's for!"

"Tape it to the window, turn it on, optical vibration plus rumbling—no way they can hear us."

"Seriously?" she inquired.

He nodded. "You gotta work with what you got."

"This is what you guys did with your downtime? Figured out *McGyver* ways to get out of sticky situations?"

Tank laughed. "Pretty much, Liz. *And you*. We talked about you."

She sat up straight. "What did Robert say?"

He waved off her question. "Nothing much. Mainly, how much he missed you."

"Do you mean sexually?"

"No! Why does your mind go there?"

She shrugged. "Well, I haven't had sex in two years, and you gave me a vibrator."

Tank spit his drink out. Grabbing at the napkin to wipe up the mess that landed on his tie, he snarled, "Why the hell do you do that to me? One minute you're all prim and proper then you say something devilish."

She snickered. "I'm glad something can still ruffle your feathers." She cut into her filet mignon. "It's good to be out with a friend again."

"I'm a friend. I'm just not the 'best girlfriend'. Keep that in mind. You can't be talking tampons and periods and vibrators in my presence."

"Hey, you're the one who brought me the vibrator."

"That isn't what it's for." He returned, chomping down on a large piece of steak. He could feel himself getting hard.

"How was I supposed to know it had more than one use?"

He pointed at her with his fork. "There, right there, there's the 'devilish'."

"Am I getting you hot and bothered?" She reached under the table and placed a hand on his knee. She wasn't sure what had come over her, but she couldn't stop.

He jerked back. "I'm not kidding, Lizzie. Don't go there."

She was suddenly embarrassed by her behavior. "I was just joking."

"We're in a tense situation, Lizzie, and I don't want you to do anything you'd regret."

Tears pricked her eyes. What the hell was wrong with her? She was flirting with her dead husband's best friend. Pathetic. "I'm sorry. I think I'm just tense." He nodded, and she got up. "I'm going to freshen up." She rushed to the ladies' room. Her face was stark white and her chest was heaving as she peered into the mirror. She splashed cold water on her wrists, trying to calm her racing heart. *I practically propositioned Tank.*

Bullshit! You've always had a thing for Tank. There's something dangerously mysterious about him. You played it safe back in the day with Robert.

"Okay, Tank is here waiting for you. You're going eat your dinner and act like nothing happened," she mumbled to her reflection.

Tank grinned when she sat down and began talking about mundane things. They finished dinner and headed home.

Tank dug up the box, and they went to the small cemetery at the edge of town to open it. Tank had already found three listening devices upstairs, which made him extremely careful. "And what better place than here?" Tank commented when Lizzie shuddered. "No one goes to a cemetery at night."

"True." Lizzie turned on the phone's flashlight and pulled out the bible. Tank practically grabbed it out of her hands. Opening it up, he crowed in delight, "A cipher. That's my boy, Robert!" He squeezed Lizzie in a one-armed hug she was sure would leave a mark.

"I'm glad you think this has the answers, but it needs a key, doesn't it?" she inquired.

"It should be in here somewhere," Tank mumbled, flipping through the pages, turning the book upside down.

"Wait!" Lizzie reached for the book. "Robert knows how I feel about books, this book specifically. I was a bit upset that he wanted you to have it, and I know these pages were never dog-eared. I would've slapped him for that."

She carefully peeled open the folded corner. "Huh. It has an 'x' on it." Doing the same to the other folded page, Robert wrote the directions to a Bible verse, "1 Chronicles 4 v 10."

"Give me that." Tank yanked it back.

"Hey!"

"That's the key, Lizzie! It's in that verse." He quickly flipped to the proper page.

"I just see the verse."

"That's right, but believe me, it's the key. We made it up when we went through basic." He stood up. "The sooner I get started, the sooner we know."

Pulling her up, he kissed her hard on the mouth. Before she could react, he let her go, taking her hand and pulling her to the car.

Chapter Three

When they arrived back at the house, Lizzie stepped inside while Tank stood at the threshold. "Are you coming in?"

"I need to take a drive, clear my head. Make sure you set the alarm."

"I'll see you when you get back?" *God, she hated how needy she sounded.*

"You'll probably be in bed."

Nasty thoughts unfurled in her brain. "Oh."

Tank hated the sadness in her eyes and pulled her close. "I'm going to get a drink and think about everything. Soon, we are going to sit down and talk about us."

Her face flamed. "Us?"

He tilted her face up. "Yes, us. Rob talked to me about a few things." He kissed her quickly and pushed her back into the house, closing the door in her face.

She prepared for bed, hoping the cool sheets against her naked body would calm her erratic thoughts, but she tossed and turned. *Did Rob want them together? Oh God, is Tank only fulfilling a promise?*

That would be horrible, to love a man who saw her as an obligation.

Finally, she fell asleep, but noise downstairs woke her. *Tank must be back.* She started to drift back to sleep, but two sets of voices floated through the air. She sat up quietly and reached over to the nightstand. A click underneath it and a thumbprint impression opened the gun case Rob had insisted on installing. She palmed the Glock and moved naked and trembling to the corner of the room. Footsteps were heading upstairs. She was ready just like Rob and Tank had shown her all those years ago. *And where the hell is Tank?* The steps stopped and the bedroom door opened.

"Well, it appears we're playing hide and seek. Come out, come out, wherever you are?" The gravelly voice made her skin crawl, but she held steady. "We don't want to hurt you; we just need what you dug up. After, we'll let you go back to sleep."

She heard the second man on the stairs. He wasn't bothering to be quiet, but no other sounds emanated from downstairs. With a steady breath, she aimed.

"Come on, lady," the second man spoke up. He was going through the closet across the room.

She glanced back and the first man was almost upon her. "There you are, all pretty and naked, too." He advanced and she shot at his kneecap. He fell back as she slammed back against the wall. She'd forgotten about the backfire.

The second man rushed from the closet, but she was steady and hit him square in the knee. They were howling in pain. Grabbing her phone from the nightstand, she jumped on the bed, avoiding the men. Flinging the French doors to the balcony open, she vaulted the side, dangling naked from the iron bars with the Glock in one hand and her phone in her mouth. She dropped softly to the ground, looking around frantically for something to cover her nakedness.

She grabbed the cushion off her bench seat and wrapped it around her as she dialed 911 and explained the situation. Her next call was to Tank. He answered on the first ring. "I need you to come home. Two intruders. I shot them. I'll probably be charged with murder, well, at the very least, assault because I hit them both like you and Robert showed me."

"Did you call the police?"

"Yes."

He swore softly. "I'll be there in two minutes. Keep talking to me."

"It's kind of hard to hold the phone and the bench cushions."

"Lizzie, you're not making any sense. Are they dead?"

"No, well, unless they bleed out. Should I check? I don't want to go up there again." She was beginning to feel a bit dizzy.

"Lizzie, listen to me. Where did you hit them?"

"The second man, I hit in the knee 'cause I had to correct for the backfire, and the first one pushed me against the wall." She sat down on the other bench. The police came in, and she pointed them to the balcony. Her stomach churned. She prayed she wouldn't throw up. "The police are here."

"I'm almost there."

Tank rushed through the garden gate moments later to find Lizzie wrapped in a bench cushion, talking to several firemen. Taking off his jacket, he growled, "Where the hell are your clothes?"

Lizzie jumped and almost dropped the cushion, correcting it quickly but not before several men saw her breasts, including Tank. He grabbed her and shoved her into his coat. "What the hell is going on here?" He glared at the men. "Not even a blanket, boys? The woman was assaulted, and it's friggin' November."

The men quickly found something else to do as Tank wrapped her in his arms and held her close. She was shaking, cold, and terrified, and he'd never been prouder. Chief Michaels walked over. "Thomas O'Leary, I never thought I'd see you back in these parts again. You here to stay?"

"For the time being."

"Should I be looking for more of this?" He nodded toward the balcony.

"I don't know what this is. You want to fill me in?"

"It appears Elizabeth had an altercation in her home with two burglars. She reacted calmly. We have the two in custody and will be transferring them to County as soon as we get them back from the hospital."

"How did it happen?" Tank glanced down at Lizzie. She quickly relayed the incident, ending with the gunfire.

"She shot one in the kneecap. The other was shot in the pecker, practically took it right off. She is one brave woman."

Tank could feel his anger boiling. They were treating it like no big deal, merely burglars breaking in. But he knew better. He'd managed to translate enough of the bible and needed to get it to Washington.

"Now, son, I can see the storm clouds brewing up in your eyes, but she's going to be fine. We're going to get this mess cleared up, probably a bunch of druggies. We've been having a little trouble with that."

"Maybe you need to take her somewhere safe for the night," The chief raised a bushy eyebrow at Tank, and he nodded. "You're not gonna be able to go in the house 'cause we gotta get forensics in there and everything."

Before Lizzie could argue that she needed clothes, she was hustled into her car, and they were rushing out of town. Tank looked at her pale face. "You really shot the guy in the dick?"

She nodded, turning and rolling down the window. Seconds later, she threw up. Tank pulled over and held her hair away from her face. When she finished, he wet a napkin with a bottle of water and wiped her mouth. "Sorry. Too soon?"

She offered a small smile. "I'm good. I just can't get it out of my mind."

"I'll get us a room."

After making sure they hadn't been followed, he pulled into a nondescript motel close to the interstate, paid cash, and ushered Lizzie into a dreary room, but at least it was clean. "Hey, it's a lot better than some places I've stayed," he reassured her.

"I suppose. There's only one bed," she pointed out.

"This wasn't exactly what I planned, Lizzie. You take the bed, I'll sleep in the chair." He opened the door once more. "I've got a bag of supplies stashed in your car. I'll be right back."

"Always prepared," she mumbled.

He glanced back at her. "Nothing could have prepared me for you naked when I got there."

She chuckled. "Well, it was either grab clothes or shoot invaders."

Tank frowned. He hadn't been there to protect her. *Damn, what the hell good am I?*

"Stop it," Lizzie ordered, reading his face. "It wasn't your fault, Tank."

"I should've planned better, but I was thinking…" He broke off and went to get the supplies.

They both knew why he left her alone.

He came back in, opened the duffle, and extracted a large shirt. "Cover yourself. I won't be going for any more drinks, and you won't be tempting me. Understand?"

"You said you needed to think up a plan, Tank."

"We both know I went for that drink to calm myself or I'd have been in your bed tonight. If I have been in your bed tonight, none of this would have happened," he snarled.

"Don't get angry with me, Tank," she retorted. "I never told you to go." She covered her mouth in embarrassment. Could she get any more desperate?

"God, Lizzie." He was on her in a flash, taking her in his arms. "I've wanted you forever, but you were always Robert's." *There, I said it.*

"Not out of pity, or obligation?"

He understood what she was asking. "No, Lizzie. If I was smart, I'd keep my mind on the job, but all I can think about is you. You're damned inconvenient if you ask me, but I want you."

Lizzie reached up and touched his face before kissing him softly. "I want you, Thomas." Stepping back, she shed his coat and stood naked.

"Lizzie," he whispered. He reached for her, tossing her onto the bed, kissing her passionately as he climbed on, crushing her into the mattress. She answered his kiss with equal fervor.

Tank quickly divested himself of his clothes. Soon, he was as naked as her. She stared at the man her body yearned for. He was a magnificent specimen of what God had intended man to be. Large arms and chest, dark curly hair on his torso tapered down to a full and thick cock. She tore her eyes away and continued down to where the scars puckered around his right thigh, where flesh became metal.

"If my leg bothers you, I can put out the light."

She scanned his face but could detect no emotion. "You are a warrior. You survived. Does it still hurt?" She leaned down to touch the gnarled flesh.

"I got nothing there, baby. The only ache I have is a little higher."

Lizzie smiled. She ran a fingernail lightly across the head of his cock. "That hurts?"

"Oh yeah. Give it a gentle rub." His head fell back as he moaned.

She continued to stroke him as he removed the metal from his thigh. He stopped her with a touch. "You're going to make me come like a teen, and I've dreamed of this for too long." He flopped down beside her, gathering her in his arms and dragging her on top of him. "Ah, God, the feel of your pussy is killing me."

He reached down between them, testing her wetness and brought the sweetness to his lips. Her essence surrounded him, combined with her moans of pleasure and his mind reeled. *His. His Lizzie.* Moving her slightly, he brought her up for another scorching kiss, then sat her upon his hard cock until she was fully embedded. Nothing had ever felt so good.

She lifted herself until she was barely touching his cock. Pleasure exploded through Tank as she began to gyrate, her breasts swaying in front of his eyes. He caught those beautiful orbs in his hands, stretching to suckle as the heat from her body continued to pulse around his cock. She was wild in her passion. He had always imagined she would be, but this was beyond his imagination. Tank could no longer contain himself. He grabbed her hips, thrusting into her faster. Lizzie rode him until she screamed in ecstasy. Her climax sent him over the edge, too. This was raw passion. His love, her desire combined to explode.

Chapter Four

Lizzie awoke to the tantalizing smell of coffee and donuts. She sat up as Tank set the yummy offering on the nightstand and gave her a quick kiss, tweaking her nipple. She yelped, "What was that for?"

"To get you up and moving. We have to get to Washington."

"What?" She noticed the darkness between the curtain opening. "What time is it, and what's this about Washington?"

"As in D.C. While you slept, I finished interpreting the cipher. Rob hid incriminating evidence against Mitchell and a few others all over the place. I can still count on a few folks at Langley. We're going to see them."

As he talked, Lizzie stuffed part of the donut into her mouth and took a healthy sip of coffee. She stood up to stretch when she finished.

"Fuck, Lizzie! Did I do that?" Tank brushed his fingers along her ribcage where welts appeared.

She twisted and looked down. "Probably not. The wrought iron bars were a bit unforgiving of my nakedness."

"Another thing I've got to thank Mitchell for," Tank groused.

"Let me shower and we can leave." She brushed past him.

"You've got two minutes. Mitchell's bound to discover he failed."

Lizzie ran into the shower and hurried through her ablutions, donning the clothes Tank had left on the toilet. How he procured those, she didn't even want to know.

She came out to Tank staring out the window. "Let's go, baby. It's a long drive to D.C."

He ushered her out to a dilapidated Chevy truck with Oregon plates. "Where's my car?"

"I traded down," he explained, helping her into the cab. "Mitchell probably knew your car and plates."

She shivered as he climbed in beside her. "I'll get the heat cranking as soon as I can. Sorry about all this."

She took his hand and squeezed. "I'm not, Tank. I'm sorry Robert's life was taken, but you and I are alive, and we're going to make sure whoever killed him pays dearly."

"Fasten your seatbelt. We've got over 800 miles to go. With a little luck, this time tomorrow, we'll be at Langley."

***

They avoided the highways when they could, picking up a road map when they stopped for a break in Indiana, and at 6:00 am they rolled down the street to the Secretary of Defense. A disgruntled guard eyed them suspiciously but rang the house. "You're lucky Mr. Secretary is an early riser."

Tank grinned. "He always was even when I did this detail, soldier."

Minutes later, they were ushered into a small room by another guard. The Secretary of Defense of the United States walked into the room not five minutes later. "Tank, you son of a bitch, how did you manage to stay alive?" he boomed as he entered.

Lizzie bristled.

"Down, Lizzie. He's one of the few good guys," Tank assured her, taking the man's hand and allowing him a friendly embrace. "Sir, this is Elizabeth Matthews. Lizzie, this is General Richard Welch."

"How are you holding up, my dear?"

She shook the man's hand. "I'm doing as well as can be expected, Sir. I'm hoping we can soon put an end to this and see justice for my husband and an end to this mess."

They sat down, and Tank explained the situation. Welch nodded in satisfaction. "I did as you asked and sent my best men out to uncover the information Robert had procured. He turned to Lizzie. "I've got to tell you, Elizabeth, your husband did a damn fine job. I'm sorry he had to forfeit his life for it." He patted her hand. "I'll make sure everyone knows that your husband was a hero."

After freshening up, Tank and Lizzie were chauffeured to Langley and ushered into a conference room with several generals, senators, and representatives. Peter Mitchell was also present. Mitchell made a motion to Lizzie but stopped when Tank pulled her close. "Seriously, O'Leary? I've known the woman as long as you have."

He turned to Elizabeth. "Tank's been trained to be a believable liar, much like your husband. It's going to pain me to bring forth the evidence I have against him."

Lizzie was outraged, but before she could respond, the Secretary of Defense walked in from a side door. Gone was the kindly gentleman she'd met earlier, he was now every inch the commander. "Gentleman, please be seated. Let's get this over with, shall we?"

Lizzie was suddenly nervous. Tank took her hand, giving it a little squeeze.

"After reviewing both sides," Welch began, "I understand the allegations. Robert Matthews was an excellent agent. But certain facts present unquestionable proof he was running heroin from the Middle East into the U. S."

Lizzie stiffened, but Tank held her hand tightly.

"However," the Commander continued, "new evidence has been brought to light."

He frowned at Mitchell. "A bible that Matthews had been known to carry with him was found to hold a cipher. When it was decoded, names, dates, and directions to hidden proof which shows that Matthews had, in fact, been on the trail of a cabal dealing drugs and human trafficking that Peter James Mitchell, his supervisor, ran."

"That's ridiculous," Mitchel blustered as the guards drew closer. "Just because a rogue agent says he decoded a book?" He pointed to Tank.

Tank growled, but Welch held up his hand. "Because I say so, Mitchell. As a matter of fact, I made up the cipher years ago. Robert and Tank were always very precise even when they were in basic under my command."

Mitchell realized the full scope of his error. "I'll still have a trial. It will be a dead man's word against mine." He struggled with the guards as they clapped him in handcuffs and led him away.

Tank shook Welch's hand. "Thank you for all you did for us. It could have gone badly if not for your intervention."

"It was my pleasure. Take care." He left the room.

Tank led Lizzie out the door. "Want to go to Aruba?"

Lizzie frowned. "I'd rather go to Scotland."

Tank laughed as they walked out into the sunshine. "Yeah, I figured."

Fallen

by

Nia Farrell

Chapter One

Saturday, 23 August 2014
Columbus, Georgia

The air-conditioning in St. Margaret's Catholic Church was on the fritz again. With temperatures edging toward one hundred outside, the inside of the confessional was at least eighty-five degrees.

Father Vincent Delaney knew the heat wouldn't bother him as much as the closeness of the walls. Confined spaces threatened to send him back to Iraq and the dirt hole where he'd been held for weeks after he was taken. He was a noncombatant but ISIS had tortured him anyway, hoping to break him, to make him betray his country and deny his God.

Ironically, he'd resisted only to be tempted to betray his vows now that he was back home. The counselor he was seeing for his PTSD had no clue that he lusted after her in his heart. But God knew.

He saw the weakness of his flesh, how he lay in his lonely bed and burned. Last night, he had masturbated to the image of her exotic face, those compassionate eyes, those perfect, plump, delectable lips.

He wanted to fist her long, dark hair and fuck her throat. Instead, he'd hand-washed another handkerchief this morning, promising himself that this was the last one yet knowing that there'd be more.

Ilsa Fischer was his obsession.

Father Andrew, the pastor of St. Margaret's, had listened to his confession and assigned him penance. Father Vincent found the feel of his rosary comforting. The rounds of *Hail, Mary's* were cathartic. Knowing his situation, Father Andrew had encouraged him to linger longer, to find solace in the arms of the Church and see if he could bear to step into the other side of the confessional after he'd had to leave the door open on his.

It was one thing to be a penitent, seeking forgiveness and absolution. But to be a confessor was to serve as God's voice on earth. It was a privilege and a responsibility that he did not feel worthy to perform with such stains upon his soul. He'd strayed far enough in his mind to feel lost. So far he hadn't managed to find his way back home. Instead, he'd been wandering like Moses in the Wilderness, helpless to help himself let alone those around him.

Father Vincent inhaled deeply, filling his lungs with the scents of incense, burned-out candles, and lemon oil wood polish rising from the rows of pews and the walnut confessional on one side of the nave. Dating from the nineteenth century, the ornate cabinet had been designed and built to suit the patron who'd paid for much of the church's construction. Solid doors ensured privacy for those seeking absolution and allowed the priest to closet himself from the world and focus on the person on the other side of the screened partition. He had used the padded kneeler when he confessed to Father Andrew, but a chair had been added for those who needed it.

God called him to notice the place of forgiveness. Compelled to answer, he reached for the confessional door.

A time-worn bench spanned the back of the space, empty, beckoning, drawing him inside. The walls started to close in. He drew a steadying breath and recited the Twenty-Third Psalm. Called to be a shepherd, he thought of his last flock and wondered how many survived.

He should pray for their souls.

And his.

Father Vincent closed his eyes and drew the door shut behind him. With his thoughts turned inward, he was able to tolerate the small space of the confessional and lift up his unit in prayer. He was asking for strength for himself when the sound of footsteps made him halt mid-thought.

The other door opened and closed, sealing the parishioner inside.

Panic gripped his chest, stealing his breath and squeezing his heart. This wasn't his parish. This wasn't his church.

He shouldn't be here. He was an imposter. An interloper. A sinner as in need of forgiveness as the other person who had come seeking it.

He'd been alone in the church when he'd entered the confessional. Whoever had come in didn't know that Father Andrew had gone. He forced himself to stay silent. If they thought that no one was here, they'd leave him alone.

If he pretended to be asleep, maybe they'd torture someone else.

Just that fast, he was back in his pit, starved, dehydrated, with flea bites and burn marks covering his skin like the plague. He swallowed a whimper, choking on it, silently keening, praying to die.

The memory of Ilsa's voice pulled him back from the hellhole of Iraq to awareness of where he was.

The walls started to close in on him again. He reached for the door, intending to apologize and flee.

"Forgive me, Father. I'm sorry. I don't know how this works."

Father Vincent froze, recognizing the silken voice that had eased him from more than one episode and had slipped him into an altered state when she'd talked him into being hypnotized. He thought that he had imagined it, but Ilsa was here, on the other side of the screen.

Ilsa was here.

He cleared the chokehold on his throat and lowered his voice to disguise it. "How long has it been since your last confession?"

"In the Church? Never," she admitted. "I'm not Catholic."

No, but her paternal grandmother was. Russell Fischer, her American-born father, was Caucasian, Cherokee, and half Panamanian—mostly Hispanic with a bit of Mayan and African-American ancestry. Her maternal grandmother was a British-born Episcopalian who'd married a Punjabi Sikh.

An exotic blend of all her bloodlines, Ilsa favored her East Indian grandfather.

"But one of my patients is. I'm a counselor."

And a damn good one. When he wasn't getting anywhere with the one at the base, he'd canvassed his friends with PTSD and one name kept popping up. Ilsa Fischer. She was a psychologist rather than a psychiatrist, but she'd been raised on Army bases around the world. Her father had retired as a one-star general before exposure to Agent Orange in Vietnam finally killed him.

"I see," he said, hesitant to dredge for information. Whatever his therapist divulged was protected by the sanctity of the confessional, but she had to abide by her conscience, professional oaths, and Federal HIPAA laws.

She was quiet for a moment. "I'm sorry. This was a bad idea."

Hearing the shift when she rose to leave, he quickly stood, desperate to keep her here. "No, wait! Please," he added, sweetening the harsh insistence of his panicked response. "It must be important, otherwise, you wouldn't have come. Please," he cajoled. "Sit. Tell me how I can help."

She sighed softly and sank onto the chair. He did the same.

"I don't know that you can. I don't know that anyone can. It's a hopeless situation."

"As long as there's life, there is hope." The platitude was so overused, he nearly cringed when it spilled from his lips. "Can you tell me why you're feeling this way?"

She inhaled a shaky breath and puffed it out, searching for the words and the courage to speak them. "It's because of who I am. Who he is. I'm his therapist. I'm attracted to him and there's nothing I can do about it. I refuse to risk my license...risk my future...on any patient, let alone someone who's unavailable."

"Unavailable?"

"Yes," she whispered. "To be with me would be a mortal sin in the eyes of the Church. He has enough that he's dealing with after his last tour in Iraq."

He'd been in Iraq. He might be dealing with it for the rest of his life.

"Even if I wasn't his therapist, he's still unavailable. Emotionally. Physically. Spiritually."

"Because you're not Catholic?

"No, because he is."

Well, that made no sense. "If you thought that there was a chance for things to work out, would you be willing to convert?"

"It can never work," she lamented. "He's...he's taken. Married," she blurted, almost as a hasty afterthought.

Married. But to whom?

Or what?

Father Vincent tamped down the urge to confront her, to demand to know if she was talking about him when he was almost certain that she was. He tried another tack. "And you refuse to be responsible for the breakup of a marriage. That is…admirable."

Admirable but not ideal. He'd prefer her to be totally honest with him. She should tell him how she felt. At least give him a chance to decide how to proceed. "Have you considered separating yourself…referring him to another therapist?"

"I have," she breathed. "I have. But we've made such headway since I started hypnosis with him. I don't want to risk losing the ground that we've gained."

Father Vincent dropped his hand to his lap and squeezed his erection. In his mind, he unzipped his pants, pulled out his cock, and jacked off into his handkerchief while she sat clueless on the other side. He still didn't know for certain that she was talking about him but hell if it didn't seem like it.

There was only one way to find out.

"Tell me about him. Does he have children? How long has he been married?"

She went quiet, thinking about how to answer. "He's married to his work," she said slowly.

"Jobs change," he challenged, unhappy that she was prevaricating. "People change."

"Some do," she parried. "And some don't. He has a vocation. A calling."

Oh, Ilsa.

It was him. He knew it. Gripping his hard-on, he envisioned her on her knees at his feet.

"Does he know how you feel?" he rasped, his pulse quickening and his respiration growing deeper with his arousal.

"No. I can't say anything without risking the rapport that we've established. He trusts me to help him. I won't make him choose."

"Choose? Between what?" he asked, pumping harder. Christ, if only he could touch her. Take her. Get this fever for her out of his system.

"Between me and his work."

"His vocation? Shouldn't he have some say in it? How do you know that he doesn't want it, too?"

"He does," she keened. "That's why I came. I suspected how he felt and asked him while he was under hypnosis. God help me. That was so unethical. But if I tell him what I did, I don't know what he'll say. How he'll feel. How he'll react. I don't want to lose him."

"I don't think you will," he said softly, hoping to reassure her. "If you're that concerned, maybe next time he's under, you could tell him just what you've told me and ask him if he wants to remember when he wakes up. Give him the choice that you've been denying him. I think he has a right to know."

His body was on fire, but his mind was burning. What had she felt so compelled to know that she'd questioned him while he was under?

"Tell me," he said. "Tell me what you asked him. Tell me what he said."

"I…um…I asked him if he liked me. He does. I asked if he thought about me outside of our sessions."

Vincent already knew the answer to that.

"I asked…" She blew out harshly. "I asked if he touched himself while he was thinking of me."

"And does he?" he asked, wanting to hear her say the words.

"Yes," she whispered, her tone colored with shame. "He said that he had to buy more handkerchiefs. He was lucky to find them on sale."

He squeezed his prick in a crushing grip, holding back his finish by sheer willpower.

"I'm sorry," she blurted, sounding agitated. "It's my problem, not yours. I just—I thought maybe I could gain some clarity coming here."

"You need to tell him."

She gave a laugh, sharp, short, and bittersweet.

"Tell him," Vincent said, his tone as firm as the grip on his cock.

"I…I can't. I'm sorry. There's too much at stake."

She rose to leave. He couldn't let her. He was out of the confessional and standing in her way when she swung open the door, intent on escape.

Her blue eyes widened. Her mouth opened, wordless. The color in her cheeks deepened.

She'd been caught, and she knew it.

There was no escaping him now.

Chapter Two

Ilsa had no right to feel betrayed but she did. Father Vincent wasn't supposed to be here. At some point, he'd figured out who she was and had known that she was talking about him. He had listened while she tried to untangle the mess in her mind and hadn't tried to stop her.

He'd just let her ramble.

The off-duty Army chaplain was dressed in civilian attire. His thick brown hair had grown since their appointment on Monday. A short beard stubbled his face. His muscled shoulders filled the width of his black summer-weight suit jacket, worn with a once-crisp white shirt that clung to his sweat-dampened chest. The zipper of his matching black slacks was being sorely tested by the weight of a massive erection.

He wanted her. If she had any doubt, the proof in his pants and the heat in his eyes dispelled it.

He pinned her with his gaze and stepped closer. "Tell me," he grated. Catching her arms and hauling her against him, he slid one hand to the small of her back and filled his other with a fistful of hair.

She gasped when he tightened his hold on her head and rocked his pelvis against her.

"Father Vincent!" she cried, pushing futilely against the sculpted wall of his chest. He'd been working hard after his rescue to get back in shape, with a goal of rejoining his unit or going wherever Uncle Sam decided to send him.

"Vincent," he grated, nipping her ear. Pulling down on her hair, he forced her chin up and brought his face close to hers. "Say it, lamb," he rasped, his voice thick with desire. "Say my name."

"V—Vincent," she croaked. "Please…"

He smiled darkly. "Tell me," he demanded again. "Tell me what you want. Tell me what you need. I can smell you, little lamb. Your panties are wet, aren't they?"

"Yes," she whispered. There was no sense trying to deny it. The air was ripe with her arousal.

Grasping her wrist, he curled her fingers over his shaft and pumped himself in her hand. "Do you want this? Tell me, Ilsa."

"Yes," she sobbed, shaking, knees threatening to buckle. "Yes. Yes, I want you. *I want you!* But I can't have you. Don't you see?"

"I see you," he murmured. "In my dreams, I see us together. Don't say you haven't imagined it, too. Imagined what it would be like."

She had. God help her, she had. Vincent was a handsome man with a beautiful, wounded soul. Iraq had left him shattered. She'd spent the last month helping him pick up the pieces.

"No one has to know but us."

And God.

Vincent was married to the Church. She was his therapist. Being together wasn't just morally wrong. It was criminal.

"It's too dangerous. If anyone finds out—"

"They won't," he insisted, silencing her protest when he slammed his mouth down on hers, claiming it with his lips, his teeth, his tongue. Lust consumed her, stealing her breath and turning her respiration ragged. Her chest heaved with effort but failed to draw in enough air, making her thighs quiver and turning her knees to jelly. She clung to him when her legs threatened to buckle.

He held her fast against him, letting her feel his desire. He groaned into her mouth, as affected by their soul-searing kiss as she was. Hearing it melted the last of her resistance.

Vincent needed her. He wanted her. After his horrific experience in Iraq, he was seeking to reaffirm his humanity and all that it entailed, including his sexuality. The logical side of her warned that she should leave. The professional side scolded her for not being stronger.

The woman in her was dangerously seduced.

"No one can know," she whispered against his lips, still tasting the hint of mint from his tongue. "It will have to be our secret."

"For now," he agreed. "If you're worried about your license, refer me to someone else."

Reaching, he thrust his hand under her skirt and pushed his fingers between her thighs.

Just like he'd thought, Ilsa was drenched.

"But your vocation," she stammered, making one last effort to talk some sense into him. "Your career…"

His lips formed a humorless smile. "My career has been in question since they pulled me from that pit in Iraq. Captivity changed me," he reminded her. "*You know this….*"

She did. God help her, she did. He'd spent hours questioning his purpose, his role, his future, wondering how he could remain in service to his country with the triggers that he had.

Ilsa fought the urge to grind her clit on his questing hand. "Whether or not you're a chaplain, you're still a priest and my patient until I can refer you."

A low growl sounded in the back of his throat. Lowering his head, Vincent adjusted his angle and claimed her mouth in a bruising kiss. The prurient thrill of something so forbidden made it all the more dangerous to her libido. She wanted him. He wanted her. Every fiber of her being warned that he would not be denied.

Not that she could. She wanted this as much as he did.

God would just have to understand.

He backed her into the penitent's side of the confessional and pulled the door closed behind them. "Step up," he growled, guiding her to stand on the prayer bench. Reaching behind her, he unzipped her skirt and let it fall to her feet. She steadied herself on his shoulder and stepped out of it.

Bending down, he picked up her skirt and tossed it over by the chair. Rising, he let his admiring eyes do a long, slow slide up her body. Lingering on the thigh-high hose and garter belt she'd worn because of the heat, he fastened his gaze on the swell of her breasts. "Take off your top."

Slipping the buttons from their holes, she shrugged her blouse free of her shoulders and tossed it on the chair.

"Christ."

Like sating their lust in this hallowed place, the single word was at once sacred and profane. Right now, even the threat of hellfire and damnation wasn't enough to stop what they had started.

He shed his coat and opened his shirt, revealing a wide, muscled chest and a taut, toned abdomen. Unable to resist the temptation, she splayed her fingers over his pecs and rubbed the pebbled tips.

Breath hissed between his teeth. He unclasped her red lace bra and bared her breasts, cupping them in his hands, molding them with his fingers, kneading her twin mounds of flesh like a potter working his clay.

Her nipples furled tight. He rolled them between his fingers and played with them, pinching, twisting, rubbing, and plucking them. Fastening his lips over one, he feasted on it like a starving man.

She supposed he was that. He might not have been with a woman in years, but the way that he touched her without hesitation made her think that he'd done this before taking the vow of celibacy that he was set on shattering.

Shoving her fingers into his hair, she held him to her breast, relishing the press of his lips, the scrape of his teeth, the lash of his tongue. He sucked her other nipple into his mouth, sending a bolt of sexual energy to strike at her core.

She was so empty, it hurt.

"Please," she whimpered.

Keeping his mouth on her breast, he hooked a finger in the crotch of her panties, parted her folds, and pushed it inside her. After months of self-imposed celibacy, one finger filled her. He had to work to stretch her out before he could fuck her with two, triggering a string of mini-orgasms that made juice trickle down her thighs.

His breaths grew harsher. Breaking away, he unfastened his belt, undid his pants, and pulled himself free.

Ilsa felt her core clench at the sight of his erection, too thick for her grip and longer than she'd ever handled. None of her previous partners came close to Father Vincent in length or in girth.

He fisted himself, working precum from the tip. Watching it drip made her mouth go suddenly dry.

She licked her lips. A low growl sounded in the back of his throat.

"Touch me," he ordered. Catching her wrist, he brought her hand to his groin. Ilsa wrapped her fingers around his shaft as far as she could reach and stroked his length with firm, practiced pulls.

"Yessss," he hissed. "That's it. So hot," he murmured. "I've dreamed of this. Your tits filling my mouth. The taste of your pussy on my tongue. Your hands on my body, touching me, stroking me. I want to feel your mouth on my cock."

Nodding, Ilsa urged him back to give her room to step down. Not letting go of her grip on his erection, she led him to the chair. Draping her blouse on the back so that she could sit, she wet her lips, opened her mouth, and leaned forward, taking him into her mouth.

He fed her his length, rubbing on her tongue and pushing against her palate, seeing just how much of him that she could take. Adjusting her angle, she took him down her throat, pulling a moan from the depths of his being. He winnowed his fingers into her hair and took control, snapping his hips and fucking her face with abandon, relishing the sounds she made and ignoring the drool that dripped between his feet.

Soon, his pattern changed. His cock swelled. The telltale harshness to his breath signaled the end was near.

The next thing she knew, he stopped with his cock down her throat deep enough to make tears burn in her eyes.

"Stand up," he growled, pulling free with an audible pop. "Stand on the kneeler and brace yourself on the back of the prie-dieu or the wall and stay there, just like that. I'll be right back."

She clutched the top of the prayer bench, thighs quivering, her body trembling with need.

Vincent returned a minute later with a vial of oil in his hand. Setting it aside, he stepped back and peeled off his shirt, tossing it onto the chair. Toeing off his shoes, he shucked his pants and added them to his pile. He poured the oil into his palm and lubricated his length, making the ruddy column of vein-roped flesh gleam in the ambient light. Pouring more on his fingers, he oiled her slit and dragged his fingers up to lube her anus as well.

Ilsa shivered to think what he might want.

What would he demand of her?

Bending his knees slightly, he took himself in hand and wet his prick on her juices. Tracing her seam with his glans, he parted her folds and pushed his way inside, inch by breathtaking inch. Jacking his hips, he drove in deeper and deeper, going until he bottomed out.

Fallen

He felt her cringe and kissed the base of her neck, squeezing her breasts and tormenting her nipples. Bracing her outstretched arms on the wall, she pushed back against him, silently begging for more.

Vincent gave it to her, thrusting into her, each stroke more powerful than the last until he was pounding into her, filling the air with the musk of arousal and the liquid sounds of sex. Reaching down, he found her clit and fanned it with his fingers, catching it between them and catapulting her to an orgasm that lasted forever.

The familiar tension built again. His movements became increasingly erratic. He shoved his thumb in her other hole. "I'm close," he grated, fucking her with desperate abandon, his double penetration making her moan. "You can swallow me or I can come in your ass. What's it going to be, lamb? Where do you want me to finish?"

She wanted him to stay where he was but she was pretty sure Father Vincent didn't carry a condom in his pocket.

"I've never done anal," she confessed. The men that she'd been with either weren't interested or she hadn't trusted them enough to try. "Just…go slow and be careful, okay?"

"Oh, lamb," he crooned, his voice stroking her like a jaguar's tongue. Pulling out, he oiled his hand

and lubed her hole, fucking her with one finger, then two, then three, stretching her out, preparing her most intimate place for his possession.

"Relax," he murmured, guiding the head of his erection to press against her pucker. "Push back on me. Open for me. Let me in, little lamb. That's it. There. That's my good girl."

He sank his length into her dark passage, dredging her channel, advancing until he was balls-deep inside her. "Fuck," he huffed, grasping her hips to lock them together. "How are you? Is it too much?"

His possession came with a new set of sensations. "I'm okay," she answered, wonder in her voice. She expected it to hurt more—and maybe it would once he got going. "But you're not moving. It burns a bit from getting stretched. I'll tell you if it gets to be too much. I know you have to move."

He was holding back for her sake. His muscles trembled with the effort. Biting the base of her neck, he tilted his pelvis back and forth, pulling partway out before pushing back in, seeing how much she could handle. He repeated his action, hunching his back and burying his cock in her ass. "I need to finish," he apologized and started pumping in earnest.

Curling her fingers into fists and clamping her jaw, she focused on staying relaxed and not tightening up. It was all she could do to handle him where no man had gone before.

"I'm coming," he grated. Burying himself to the root, he exploded inside her, his body heaving as he emptied himself in her depths. He held himself there for a minute more, loathe to let her go.

"Stay here."

She winced when he pulled out, amazingly still half-hard. Reaching for his jacket, he pulled out two handkerchiefs. She arched a brow at the spare. He grinned unapologetically. "I was a scout," he told her, tucking one in her crack and using the other to clean himself. "Always prepared. And before you overthink it, carrying two handkerchiefs is something I learned early on. My mentor always had a second to share when he was ministering to others. He rarely got them back."

"I'll wash it and return it to you," she promised, grateful that he'd had them. She'd never thought that she'd do a walk of shame out of a church confessional.

"Or you can keep it for next time," he murmured against her shoulder, kissing it before he stepped away again, intent on getting dressed. The space was so cramped, she stayed balanced on the prie-dieu and watched him layer himself.

Slipping on his jacket, Vincent cupped her face and gave her a kiss. "I'll wait for you outside. Get dressed and think about where you'd like to eat dinner. I seem to have worked up an appetite."

When he reached to adjust himself, the lambency in his blue eyes was unmistakable. He was hungry, all right, and for more than just food.

But what happened here couldn't happen again.

Not until they were free to pursue it.

Chapter Three

The heat inside the church was oppressive. Outside, it was worse. Vincent walked Ilsa to her car after she promised to meet him for dinner.

She insisted that they drive separately.

He wasn't certain that she would show.

His poor lamb. She was as confused by what happened as he was certain. Making love to her had triggered an epiphany. He'd already felt a driving need for change, had prayed long and hard for Divine guidance. This afternoon, he realized that he could still serve God as a layperson—military or civilian. For the first time since Iraq, he was filled with hope for the future...one spent with Ilsa at his side.

Now if he could make her see it.

He arrived at Rick's, a *Casablanca*-themed dinner club, fifteen minutes ahead of their reservation. Ilsa appeared at seven o'clock on the dot, wearing a sleeveless black sheath dress. Her dark hair was long and loose. Her perfectly applied makeup bought out the blue in her eyes. She'd applied vibrant pink lipstick to her supple, expressive mouth.

Remembering how her lips had felt around his cock, he took a deep breath and willed his body to behave.

He greeted her with a welcoming smile. "Glad you could make it," he told her. "You look beautiful."

Beautiful and apprehensive and struggling with guilt. *For letting him fuck her in the confessional?* he wondered, *or letting him fuck her at all?* No matter. By the end of the evening, he hoped to help her move past a scandalous beginning and into a socially acceptable future. He wanted to show her how good things could be. How good *they* could be together. He wanted to worship her body and kiss those tempting lips while her taste was still on his tongue.

Her nostrils flared on an intake of breath. Realizing how he must look, he schooled his features and willed his cock to stand down—not the easiest thing to do when he remembered what it was like to be buried in her warmth.

They were shown to a quiet, private table in the back, thanks to his friendship with Rick's owner. The menu featured an eclectic mix of Moroccan, American, and French cuisine. Deciding on dishes made with beef, Vincent ordered a bottle of red wine for them, hoping that a little alcohol might help ease the tension still emanating from her.

"Cheers," he said, lifting his first glass of wine. Ilsa rotely lifted her goblet. "To good food, good wine, and good company."

The clink of crystal seemed to crack the wall of ice surrounding her. His words coaxed the first real rays of warmth that he'd seen since she arrived.

"I'm glad you came," he told her. "I wanted you to be the first to know. I'm mustering out."

She stared at him, speechless, her blue gaze as intense as during their weekly therapy sessions when she was watching for triggers, seeing how far he could get before one of them kicked in.

"I think I've known since Iraq that it's time to move on. I have another year left on my contract. I don't know if I can get a medical discharge, but I know I'll be a detriment to my unit if we end up in a combat zone. They need someone they can depend on, who'll stand strong beside them when things get tough. Right now, that's not me."

Ilsa took another sip of liquid courage and angled her head. "I know that we've covered what happened to you there. I'd like you to tell me what brought you to that point. What attracted you to the Army? What drew you to the priesthood?"

Vincent swiped a hand across his face and rubbed the back of his neck. "Remember the scout thing? The summer before my senior year of college, my little brother was working on a history badge. I took him to Antietam Battlefield. We were walking down the Bloody Lane toward the tower and the monument for Thomas Meagher and the Irish Brigade. All of a sudden, I found myself in the middle of the fray. The air was thick with the smell of black powder and the fog of battle. I saw flames shoot from the ends of Confederate muskets and watched men in blue wool uniforms get mowed down in ranks. Hearing their screams, I started yelling, 'Help the wounded! Help them! They're dying!' And a voice…in my head…in my heart, told me to save the fallen.

"Save the fallen," he repeated. "Not the wounded. Not the dying. In that moment, I felt that I was being called to save the souls of those who've fallen from grace. Because of my vision, I interpreted it as the souls of soldiers and entered the seminary with the express intent of becoming a chaplain. But I see so many other souls—civilians—in need of redemption, I'm rethinking my initial conviction."

"But your commission. The priesthood. What happens if you leave one or both of those behind?"

It was a question that he'd been struggling with since his rescue. After being with Ilsa today, he'd realized that he had been praying all wrong. Instead of asking for healing that would let him return to duty, he needed to heal enough to get on with his life, whatever that entailed, wherever God's hand might lead him.

He angled his head and turned his stemware, making wine swirl in the bowl. "I move on," he said simply. "There are far more laypeople than priests doing God's work here on earth."

Ilsa looked concerned. "But where will you go? What will you do?"

"There's always my parents' basement." He wished he was joking but without a job to pay expenses, he might not have a choice. "I'm considering going back to school," he told her. "Getting my Master's in business and learning new skills. If I studied architecture…construction… carpentry…I could start a not-for-profit and build houses for homeless vets. A different sort of saving the fallen, helping vets who have fallen on hard times. I think that's something that I would be happy doing. I'm willing to entertain suggestions. No?"

Ilsa always had something to say. The perfect response. Insightful observations.

Tonight, he'd rendered her speechless.

"Enough about me," he said smoothly, needing to fill the uncomfortable silence. "I want to hear about you. What were you like as a child? What did you first want to be when you grew up?"

Ilsa smiled softly and shook her head. "After seeing a Civil War reenactment, I wanted to ride horses, swing sabers, and shoot cannons. My dad was all for it. My mother wanted me to be a ballerina. Dance lessons won. But back then, roles went to the girls who fit the look. I didn't," she said wistfully, blinking to erase the remembered hurt in her eyes.

Her multiracial, multicultural background had given her a rare beauty and a unique empathy but she would never blend in. He was fine with that. To him, she was the most beautiful flower in God's garden.

Vincent asked her more questions about siblings, cousins, where she'd gone to school, and friends that she'd kept in touch with. He didn't ask about her first love or former boyfriends, hoping to steer the conversation back to the two of them and where they might go from here.

He never quite managed it before dinner was done and the music had started. "Do you tango?" he asked. "Foxtrot? Waltz?"

She rolled her eyes and grimaced. "Yes. When my teacher made it clear that I would never be chosen for the lead ballerina, my mother made me switch to ballroom dancing. Lucky me, I had the look for Latin."

Scooting back his chair, Vincent stood and held out his hand. "Dance with me."

She hesitated, but the lure of the music proved too great. Pulling her to her feet, he led her onto the dance floor where couples with skill levels from novice to expert were waltzing. He made a frame with his arms. She stepped into it, placing her right hand in his outstretched one and settling her other hand on his shoulder.

He slid his free hand behind her back. Gooseflesh rippled across her skin, and she inhaled deeply. Centering herself, she followed his lead, moving seamlessly with him, gliding and twirling across the floor.

"You've had lessons," she whispered, sounding impressed.

"My mother insisted," he told her, glad now that she had. The jocks at school had made fun of him, but he was as much an athlete as any of them. Once the football coach had seen how he moved, he'd been recruited as a running back.

They'd won the state championship his senior year. He'd gone to college on a football scholarship, completing three years of a business major before entering the seminary.

The song ended. Some couples went back to their seats. Others joined the dancers. The small orchestra struck up the next tune.

A rumba.

Hearing it, Ilsa tried to pull away, bent on escape. Vincent refused to let her go. Pulling her against him, they began the dance of love.

With the right partner, the rumba and Argentine tango were as close to sex on a dance floor as you could get. And Ilsa was perfect for him. The heat they generated was palpable. He felt the eyes of the dancers and diners on them as they moved across the floor to the Latin beat.

When the last note faded, he was hard and she was pliant.

She let him follow her home.

They were barely in the door when he backed her against the wall, rucked up her dress, dropped to his knees, and ate her out. Replacing his tongue with one finger, then two, he lashed her clit, laving and teasing it, finally pulling it into his mouth and wringing the first orgasm from her. Her body stiffened. Short, sharp breaths burst from her lips. She came with a cry, grinding her pussy against his mouth and drenching him with her juices.

Desperate to be inside her, Vincent unzipped his fly and pulled out his erection. Lifting her up, he impaled her on his cock and banged her against the foyer wall. She clung to him with her legs wrapped around his hips and her arms clutching his shoulders.

He felt his balls draw up tight, ready to unload, when he realized he hadn't wrapped up.

"I don't have a condom on," he rasped against her neck. "Are you protected?"

"I take shots," she gasped when he bottomed out. "Come in me, Vincent."

He thrust again and climaxed in her welcoming warmth, bathing her cervix and filling her with his seed. His hips bucked as he emptied himself, shuddering to a finish.

Feeling her fingers play with his hair, he drew back his head and met her lambent gaze. "We need a bath," he murmured, unable to apologize when he wasn't the least bit sorry.

"What about a shower?"

He shook his head. "I want to hold you," he confessed. "Bathe you. Tuck you in bed and rock you to sleep. I want to spend the night with you in my arms and have you for breakfast in the morning. If I stay, that's what's going to happen."

Ilsa's answer was to curl her fingers in his hair and pull him to her for slow, wet kisses that peppered their trail up the stairs.

Vincent didn't know what tomorrow would hold or the next day or the next. He was in strange territory here, without a map and only a vague sense of how to proceed. But one thing he knew. He wanted Ilsa in his life, building a future that he'd never dared to dream of.

A future together, with her.

To be continued…

Meet the Authors

Pamela Ackerson

Debra Parmley

Teri Riggs

Maggie Adams

Nia Farrell

Pamela Ackerson

International and Amazon bestselling author, and time traveling adventurer, Pamela Ackerson was born and raised in Newport, RI where history is a way of life. She lives on the Space Coast of Florida where everyone is encouraged to reach for the stars! A hop, skip, and jump from Disney World and fun-filled imagination and fantasy.

She writes non-fiction, WW2, inspirational, self-help marketing and advertising, historical fiction, time travel, westerns, Native American, and children's preschool/first reader books.

PamelaAckerson.com
@PamAckerson
Facebook.com/PamelaAckersonAuthor
Amazon.com/Pamela-Ackerson

Debra Parmley

Debra Parmley is a best-selling, multi-genre author with twenty-three books out. She writes military romantic suspense, contemporary and holiday romance, a dystopian romance trilogy, paranormal romance, historical romance, fairy tale romance, and poetry.

She is a professional speaker and a world traveler who often brings home folk tales and music from the countries she has visited. Debra is the founder of Shimmy Mob Memphis, a chapter of the international organization which raises funds for local domestic abuse shelters. For the past twenty years, she and her husband have lived just outside Memphis, Tennessee.

Her five favorite things are shooting primitive archery with her Mongolian horse bow, shooting long guns, shooting pool, walking on the beach, and hearing from her readers. Each card and letter is a joyful treasure, like finding that perfect shell on the beach.

DebraParmley.com
@DebraParmley
Facebook.com/AuthorDebraParmley
Amazon.com/Debra-Parmley

Teri Riggs

Teri Riggs is a USA Today Bestselling author. As a child, Teri made up her own bedtime stories. When her children came along, Teri always tweaked the fairy tales she told her daughters, giving them a bit more punch and better endings when needed.

Now she spends her days turning ideas into romance books. She lives in Marietta, GA with her husband and two spoiled puppies who think they rule the world. Teri believes being married over 40 years, qualifies her as an expert in happily-ever-afters.

Teri-Riggs.com
@TeriLRiggs
Facebook.com/Teri-Riggs
Amazon.com/Teri-Riggs

Maggie Adams

Maggie Adams is an international and Amazon Bestselling romance author. Her first book in the Tempered Steel Series, *Whistlin' Dixie*, debuted in Amazon's Top 100 for Women's Fiction, humor, on November 2014. Since then, she has consistently made the Amazon best seller 5-star list with her books.

Her Tempered Steel Series has launched the tiny town of Grafton, Illinois, into international recognition with sales in Mexico, Ireland, Scotland, Australia and the UK and her follow-up paranormal series, Legends, looks to do the same!

She is the recipient of the Dayreader Reviews Best of 2015 for *Leather and Lace*, the Readers Favorite Award for *Something's Gotta Give* in 2016, the Indie Romance Convention Romantic Comedy Award 2017 for *Forged in Fire* and the 2017 New Apple Awards nomination - Suspense for *Cold as Ice*.

MaggieAdamsBooks.com
@AuthrMaggieAdms
Facebook.com/MaggieAdamsBooks
Amazon.com/Maggie-Adams

Nia Farrell

International Bestselling Author Nia Farrell is a four-times Golden Flogger Finalist and founding member of the Wicked Pens. A multi-genre writer published in nonfiction, poetry, music, articles, and children's books, she has one documentary screenplay under her literary belt and penned the one of The 50 Best Indie Books of 2016. She started writing romance at her husband's suggestion and has been published in erotic romance since 2015. She also writes as Erinn Ellender Quinn and Ree L. Diehl.

NiaFarrell.Wordpress.com
Facebook.com/NiaFarrellAuthor
@AuthrNiaFarrell
Amazon.com/Nia-Farrell

Dear Reader,

Writing this anthology was fun for all of us. As far as we know, there aren't any other anthologies with a graduated romance heat level. The idea is definitely a unique one and written for your delightful entertainment.

We hope you enjoyed the *Wounded Heroes Anthology* as much as we loved writing the stories. A short review posted on Amazon, Goodreads, or even a short note from you would be greatly appreciated

Thank you.
Pamela Ackerson, Debra Parmley, Teri Riggs,
Maggie Adams, and Nia Farrell

Made in the USA
Lexington, KY
08 November 2019

56618125R00117